Hannah's Heart

by Marnie L. Pehrson

First Edition 2005

Published by CES BUSINESS CONSULTANTS
Copyright 2004, 2005 Marnie L. Pehrson
Cover photo from Microsoft ClipArt Gallery Online
All Rights Reserved.

www.MarniePehrson.com
www.CleanRomanceClub.com

Printed in the United States of America

ISBN: 0-9729750-6-3

Chapter One

Ephraim Marston tugged the rope with all his might, but the gray mule on the other end wouldn't budge. It rested stubbornly on its hindquarters as if it planned to light there until winter, and it was only June. He'd been attempting to remove the animal for nearly half an hour. Wrapping the rope around his gloved hands one more time, he threw his weight into it and leaned completely back, the muscles in his arms flexing beneath his rolled-up shirtsleeves. With Ephraim's full weight slanted away from the animal, the stubborn mule finally decided to cooperate, and Ephraim's boots scrambled beneath him. He fell hard on his rear end and a cloud of dust billowed around him. The mule loomed over him and Ephraim could have sworn he perceived a mocking twinkle in the animal's eye.

"You good for nothin', insolent old biddy," he grumbled at the mule as he rose to his feet and slapped his gloved hands against the seat of his pants.

Hannah Jamison peered out the store window, observing the disgruntled farmer as he sauntered away from the livery stable, grumbling as he led the mule down the dusty road and periodically rubbed the smart from the seat of his denims. Hannah's blue eyes twinkled merrily and a soft giggle erupted from her full lips as she slipped a stray strand of golden blonde hair back behind her ear.

"Here's the items your mother wanted, Miss Jamison," the owner of the mercantile called to her from behind the store counter.

"Thank you, Mr. Gothard," she approached the counter, took some money from her purse and handed it to the man who gave her a bulging gunnysack.

"That's quite heavy. Would you like me to send Adam along with you to carry it home?" Mr. Gothard offered and his dark-haired wiry son appeared on cue from the back of the storeroom, put both hands to the sides of his head and slicked down his oily hair. It did little good, for as soon as he removed his hands, a cowlick sprung erect once more.

"I'd be happy to help you carry it home, Miss Jamison," the young man agreed as he wiped the excess hair tonic onto the lapels of his suit.

"That's quite all right. Thank you, but I can manage just fine," the corners of Hannah's lips turned up slightly and she retreated for the door, carrying the heavy sack along with her. Surprised at the weight of it, the sack tugged at her arms. She wasn't able to mask the fact that it would be a chore to lug it a mile back to her home.

"See there, it's just plum too heavy for ya, Miss Jamison. I'd be more'n happy to heft it for ya," the young man offered again, this time putting out his hands to take the sack.

"Really, I can manage," she shifted the bag cradling it in both hands.

"You sure?" Mr. Gothard questioned.

4

"I'm sure. Thank you very much for offering," she smiled broadly and pretended that the load wasn't too much for her. She left the establishment and turned right.

After continuing for a block or two she craned her head around and peered back over her shoulder to confirm that Adam Gothard hadn't followed her. He gave her the willies and made shopping at the mercantile a thing of little enjoyment. She continued forward with her head turned back to the mercantile.

"Umph," grunted the tall, solid mass she'd run into. Startled, Hannah lost control of the sack and it slipped from her hands onto the ground.

"Watch where you're a goin'," the man grumbled and then winced as the fifty pound feed sack he carried slipped from his hands onto his foot.

"Dad blammit!" he exclaimed as he kicked the sack off his foot and rubbed at his boot.

"I'm terribly sorry," Hannah offered apologetically as she hurriedly picked up her sack and then gazed up into the striking hazel eyes flecked with emerald green. "I didn't mean to..." she stammered.

"Of course you didn't mean to," he grumbled, still rubbing his toe. "You never mean to." He held his boot melodramatically and Hannah half expected him to pull off his shoe right there in the middle of the sidewalk and start massaging his wounded toes.

"You had your head in the durn clouds again, didn't ya, girl?" he accused.

"No, sir, I just looked back over my shoulder for a moment and then there you were. Where did you come from, anyway?" she rose to her feet, hefting her bag of merchandise.

Ephraim Marston tossed the sack of grain over his shoulder. "Where do you suppose?" he quipped, anger starting to subside from his eyes as he brushed his tousled sandy-blonde hair to the side.

Hannah's eyes darted to her right and saw farmers milling around in the feed store.

"You could have watched where you were going when you came out of the store," she defended.

"You're the one who ran into me, Miss Jamison," Ephraim flung the sack on the back of the mule and strapped it in place. "Accidents are accidents, but you have more of 'em than anybody I ever did see."

"I said I'm sorry, Mr. Marston. I'll see that I steer clear of you in the future so that my mishaps don't inconvenience you further."

"Good, you do that," Ephraim tugged at his mule and it followed him willingly down the road.

"Humph," Hannah huffed. *That man's even more stubborn than that mule of his. And to think I almost felt sorry for him!*

If she hadn't been carrying such a heavy load, Hannah would have taken the long way home which wouldn't have required her following Ephraim Marston and his mule. But since she figured she'd do well to get it home at all, she was forced to trail him while putting as much distance as possible between herself and the ornery man.

Hannah found herself chuckling occasionally as he wiggled his sore foot and rubbed at the seat of his pants.

Then she'd force herself to shift her eyes elsewhere – onto the wildflowers, the fluffy white clouds in the crystal clear azure sky, or the cows grazing in the lush green pastures. Then again, magnetically her eyes would fall to the seat of Ephraim's dusty denims. The man could fill out a pair of jeans quite nicely, and much to Hannah's chagrin she felt that odd twinge of attraction.

Why she found him fascinating was beyond her comprehension. Sure, his brawny arms, muscular legs and those unusual eyes set against his thick sandy blonde hair gave him an irresistible boyish quality in contrast to his manly physique. The combination would turn any girl's head – at least any girl who found rugged manliness with a twist of boyishness attractive. But all of that had to be laid aside when a young woman with an ounce of brains in her head weighed it against his constant cantankerous temperament. But even Hannah had to admit that he wasn't irritable with everyone.

As a matter of fact, he could be quite congenial in the mercantile or the feed store or even when haggling for the best price for his butter and eggs. His support and generosity toward his neighbors did not go unnoticed by Hannah either. If anyone were in trouble, they could always count on Ephraim to be one of the first to help them in their hour of need. On more than one occasion when Hannah took food to old widow Johnson, she'd found Ephraim there patching the woman's roof or mending her fence. Once when a deadly flu epidemic ravaged the entire community in the dead of winter, Ephraim made soup and carried it around to his neighbors. Many could attribute their lives to Ephraim's care, for they had no other way to feed themselves in their weakened state.

It was primarily Hannah who put him out of sorts. She knew he perceived her as a childish klutz always getting in his way. There was the time she let his bull out of the pen by accident. She had gone after her stray kitten by opening his fence instead of climbing over it. Ephraim spent three hours tracking down the animal before finally mustering it back to its corral. Then there was the fall social a year and a half ago when she tripped and spilled punch all over Ephraim and Rachel Merryweather. Everyone knew that Ephraim was sweet on Rachel, but after that incident, nothing materialized between the couple. Hannah knew that Ephraim blamed her for his loss.

Rachel hadn't taken it well at all and dove into Hannah with every insult she could muster. Mortified at having made a fool of herself again in front of Ephraim Marston at the social event of the season, Hannah fled the building in tears. Her brother told her that Ephraim had tried to find her afterward, but she had already gone home, tossed herself on her bed and cried herself to sleep. He probably wanted to scold her for being such a dolt and ruining his evening. For nearly three months she avoided him, walking in the opposite direction whenever she saw him.

After nearly a half a mile, the load grew too heavy for Hannah and she decided to put it down and rest for a spell. Noting a fallen log on the side of the road, she set the sack on the ground and rested on the log under the shade of a willow. She closed her eyes and leaned her head on her hands, her elbows on her knees. The afternoon sun had caused her to perspire and she opened her eyes to retrieve her handkerchief from her purse. Instead of the road and pasture before her, she looked straight into the muscular torso and forearms of Ephraim Marston.

Hannah's eyes focused on his bronze arms, his white sleeves rolled up to the middle of his biceps. Her eyes traveled to his broad chest, his white button up shirt tucked into his jeans with one suspender strapped around his shoulder and the other hanging limp at his thigh.

His hand was extended toward her with his fingers opening and closing against his palm with a welcoming motion, "Gimme that bag, girl."

Timidly, Hannah's eyes lifted to his face, apprehensive as to whether she'd find friendliness or fury in his eyes. When she saw the softened expression of his features and the golden and emerald flecks in his eyes she knew she wouldn't be scolded at that particular moment.

"That's too heavy for you. Annabelle's got some room on her back yet." When she didn't respond, he leaned over and picked up the sack and strapped it atop his mule. Hannah watched his arms work to affix the load and he turned and stretched out his hand to help her up.

One minute he infuriated her and the next her palms had gone to perspiring and every coherent thought had escaped her mind. All she could do was stare at him.

He shook his palm, "Come along, I ain't gonna bite cha."

She discretely clutched at the folds of her skirt to dry her palms before slowly slipping her hand into his. It didn't

9

take more than a few moments for her to ascend to her feet and Ephraim to release her hand, but in those moments, a picture flashed into Hannah's mind of the two of them walking hand-in-hand through his pasture on a refreshing spring afternoon.

He dropped her hand and they walked side-by-side with Annabelle trailing behind. Neither had said a word for a couple minutes when Hannah finally broke the nervous silence.

"Thank you for your help," she glanced at him. He was a foot taller than her and Hannah was five foot five herself.

"You're welcome," he nodded with his eyes still facing forward.

There was a long pause then Ephraim took a deep breath, "Sorry I fussed at ya back there. I suppose I should o' been watchin' where I was goin' myself."

"It was my fault, I was looking back toward the mercantile."

"Interested in Mr. Gothard's boy – are ya?" a slight smirk crept across Ephraim's lips.

"Where in the world did you get such a notion?" Hannah retorted rolling her eyes.

"So you ain't denyin' it then?" he teased.

"Pardon me?" Hannah stopped and thrust her hands to her hips.

He went a step further and then turned about to face her. "You didn't deny it. You just want to know where I heard it."

"Arrgggh, you are the most infuriating man!" Hannah huffed and then made to briskly sidestep around him. Just as she would have passed him, he stretched his arm out and caught her bringing her to a halt.

"So it's true, you fancy Adam?" his eyes grew more serious as they caught hers.

"You've got to be kidding me?" Hannah rolled her eyes in disgust. "He gives me the shivers."

Ephraim stepped closer to Hannah so that her eyes were only a few inches from his chest. He stood so close that she had to crane her neck to meet his gaze. His voice grew deep, even a bit provocative as his eyes fell to her lips, "Would those be bad shivers or good shivers?"

Hannah swallowed the excess moisture which had suddenly appeared in her mouth. "He repulses me," she whispered as her eyes fell to the toothpick between Ephraim's lips.

"I guess I was misinformed then," he turned away from her and started down the road.

"Who told you such a thing?" she asked as she caught up with him.

"His pa said you were sweet on Adam and well, after today, I thought maybe you were."

"No, I can assure you that I am *not* sweet on Adam Gothard," Hannah grimaced as if she'd just taken a bite of a sour lemon.

Ephraim changed the subject, "So what book are you reading these days, Miss Hannah?"

"*A Tale of Two Cities*," she replied and Ephraim, who had read the book himself, engaged her in an amiable conversation on the novel. They compared thoughts on the book until Hannah pointed to her left.

"Here's my road if you want to give me my sack."

"I'll just walk you the rest of the way."

"You don't have to do that," she assured but was flattered nonetheless.

"I know. I need to talk with your father about somethin'," he pointed to the house with his toothpick and then stuck it back between his lips.

"Oh," she sighed. *Figures,* she thought.

When they reached the house, Ephraim unstrapped the sack of goods from Annabelle's back and carried it into the large house. The Jamison's were quite well off, Mr. Jamison being the mayor of the small Tennessee village. The cream-colored house boasted a wrap-around porch, with dormer windows on the second floor.

Mrs. Anna Jamison greeted them as they entered and motioned to her left for Ephraim to place the sack on the kitchen table.

"Thank you for helping Hannah home with that, Mr. Marston," she expressed and then turned to her daughter who entered behind him. "I'm sorry, Hannah, I guess I didn't think about how hard it would be for you to carry all of that."

"That's all right, Mama. I only had to carry it halfway before Mr. Marston offered to put it on his mule's back."

"Is Mayor Jamison around, Ma'am? I need to speak with him on a matter of business," Ephraim asked.

"Yes, he's around here somewhere, just head in that direction and you should run into him," she pointed down the hall and Ephraim proceeded onward.

"I wonder what business he has with Father?" Hannah mumbled more to herself than to her mother.

Anna Jamison answered anyway, "Never you mind. Come along with me; we have work to do." With that, Hannah trailed off behind her mother.

Inside Harold Jamison's study, twelve-year-old Joshua hid behind a couch, clutching a large bullfrog. His blonde hair frazzled this way and that from the perspiration spiking his hair and dripping down his sideburns.

"How can I help you, Mr. Marston?" Harold Jamison entered his study with Ephraim just behind him and then shut the door. The stout man took a seat behind his desk and motioned for Ephraim to sit opposite him. Ephraim remained standing.

"Mayor, I came to check on that matter we discussed last month. The time is drawing closer and as you might expect, I am anxious to hear your decision."

"Yes, yes, please be seated, Mr. Marston."

Hesitantly, Ephraim sat on the edge of the chair.

"I've considered the matter and I feel you just don't have the qualifications we're looking for."

Ephraim's eyes widened and his pulse quickened, "May I ask what qualifications I lack, sir?"

"We're looking for someone younger. You are getting on up there in years, Ephraim."

"I'm only twenty-three, sir. I'd hardly call that ancient!"

"I know, I know... but someone younger would be more suitable. We want someone young with promise and connections."

Ephraim sniffed back a half-chuckle, "Good luck finding someone like that around here."

"Actually, I've already found a fine match."

"Who?" Ephraim asked incredulously.

"Not that it's really any of your concern, Mr. Marston, but since this decision does affect you, I'll be kind and answer that question."

Ephraim waited expectantly for the answer.

"Adam Gothard is a fine young man," Mr. Jamison laced his fingers together and placed his hands resolutely on the desk in front of him.

"Adam Gothard?" Ephraim bellowed and rose to his feet.

"Shh—shh," Mayor Jamison looked side to side as if he expected listening ears to come rushing out of the bookshelves.

"Adam Gothard?" Ephraim whispered incredulously. "You think Adam Gothard is a better man than me?" Ephraim thumped his chest with his thumb.

"Now, settle down, Mr. Marston, I didn't say he was a better man, just a more suitable choice." When Ephraim opened his mouth to retort, Mr. Jamison cut him off, "I expect you to stand by my decision and let this matter drop."

Ephraim's chest heaved with indignation. "I can't believe this," he ran his fingers through his tousled hair.

"Believe it, Marston. It's my decision, and it stands."

"When?" Ephraim asked.

"Spring."

Ephraim said not another word but turned to the door and stomped out of the house.

Mayor Jamison slowly made his way to the front door and stood at the screen watching Ephraim lead his mule down the dusty road to his farm across the way.

"I take it you told him?" Anna put her hand on her husband's shoulder.

"I did," the mayor nodded affirmatively, his eyes still on Ephraim whose stubborn brisk walk had shifted to a slightly slumped-shouldered dejected pace.

"Are you absolutely certain, he's not the better choice?" Anna whispered.

The mayor turned to his wife and nodded affirmatively. "Absolutely certain." Then, he left her side and traveled resolutely toward his study.

Joshua let the back door slam behind him as he clutched his frog and sought out his sister in the garden.

Hannah lifted her head from hoeing around the tomatoes. "Hi, Joshua," she greeted. "Where have you been?"

"Bubba got loose in the house again, and I had to find him," he answered.

"I thought Dad told you to keep that frog out of the house," she reminded.

"I just took him in for a minute to get myself a drink of lemonade, and he got loose. Finally found him in Dad's study."

"Oh no! Did you get in trouble?"

"No, I hid behind the couch when Dad was talkin' to Mr. Marston and then snuck out when they left. Luckily, he didn't see me."

"That's good," Hannah hesitated for a moment and then continued in a softer tone, "So you overheard their whole conversation?"

"Sure did," Joshua nodded dramatically.

"So tell me, what was it about?"

"Hmmm," Joshua scratched his head pensively as if he were weighing a matter of grave concern. "For that kind of juicy information, I might be needin' a plug o' licorice." He cut his eyes at her knowingly.

"You're rotten, you know that?" Hannah affected disgust but humor gleamed in her eyes as she reached into her apron and pulled out a plug of licorice and handed it to him. Joshua took a bite.

Hannah knelt down to pull some weeds that were closer to the tomatoes and Joshua perched himself on a stump, still holding his bullfrog under one arm and his licorice in his other hand.

Joshua lowered his voice to a secretive whisper, "Seems Mr. Marston wants a job Dad has that'll start in the spring. But Dad just told him that he can't have it. Says he thinks another man would be better for it - someone younger, with connections and - what was it he said? Oh yeah, promise."

"And who would that be?" Hannah coaxed.

"You ain't gonna believe it," Joshua shook his head emphatically.

"Who?"

"Adam Gothard!"

"No!" Hannah retorted incredulously.

"Yep, that's what Dad said. Said he thought Adam Gothard was the better man for the job."

"I just can't believe it!" Hannah gasped.

"Me neither! Bubba would be a better man for the job than Adam Gothard!" Joshua held up his frog to accentuate the point.

"So how did Mr. Marston take the news?"

"He was mad. He stormed out of Dad's office and down the road. I don't know if he was more disappointed about not gettin' the job or that Gothard was the one that beat him out of it."

"Poor Ephraim," Hannah muttered under her breath and shook her head in disappointment.

"Poor Ephraim?" Joshua's mouth dropped a little. "I thought you didn't like Mr. Marston?"

"It's not that I don't *like* him, it's just that he – he can just be so exasperating at times."

"I think you're sweet on 'im," Joshua's eyes lit up with sudden understanding.

"Oh, nonsense! Either help me with these weeds or run along and do somethin' with that frog."

Unwilling to work, Joshua trotted off toward the creek.

Chapter Two

The summer passed swiftly and soon autumn arrived. Adam Gothard had finally figured out that he should cut his hair short instead of using hair tonic to tame his unruly cowlicks. His mother had also fattened him up a bit over the summer and he wasn't quite as repulsive, but he still made Hannah uneasy.

"You goin' to the fall social with anyone, Miss Jamison?" Adam asked as he handed Hannah her merchandise over the counter.

Hannah took a deep breath and searched her imagination for some way to get out of what she felt sure was coming next. "I decided I'd like to go with my family this year instead of anyone in particular."

"Well, then, maybe I'll just do the same, and we can spend some time together," Adam nodded as if it were a plan.

Hannah gulped, that wasn't what she wanted at all. Suddenly, she wished anyone other than Adam Gothard would ask her so that she would be out of his grasp.

"I best be on my way," she ignored his comment, took her sack and briskly left the mercantile.

Upon entering the sunlight, she spotted Ephraim sitting across the street outside the livery whittling a stick to a fine point. He smiled and nodded at her. She returned the gesture. If she had the courage, she'd march right over there and convince Ephraim that it was his idea to take her to the social, but she knew she lacked both the nerve and the manipulative ability. Instead she just turned and headed home. She'd traveled about a half a mile, when Ephraim's buggy came alongside her.

"Mornin' Miss Hannah," he greeted and tipped his hat.

"Good morning, Mr. Marston," she smiled and kept walking.

"Would you care for a ride?" he patted the seat beside him.

"Well – I – I hate to inconvenience you," she stammered.

"No inconvenience, Miss," he stopped the buggy and hopped down to help her with her bag and assisted her in climbing into the conveyance. After he'd seated himself, he cracked the reins and the buggy lurched forward.

Hannah mustered her nerve, "Are you going to the fall social with anyone, Mr. Marston?"

"Nope, not this year," he shook his head negatively.

"But you will be there, won't you?"

"Don't know. Haven't decided yet."

"But you have to come, everyone will be there and you'll be missed if you stay home."

"Really? And who would be missin' an old ornery goat like me?"

"Oh, lots of people," she shrugged nonchalantly.

"Huh, I didn't know I was that popular," he snickered. "What about you? Who are you going with?" he asked.

"Just my family," she answered, holding her breath in hopes that by some miracle he might actually ask her to go with him.

He nodded understandingly and then he changed the subject and asked her about her family and about the books she had recently read. Hannah enjoyed discussing books with Ephraim. He was the only man in town that she knew of who even cared to read a book or could carry on an intelligent conversation about one.

When they reached her road, he stopped the buggy at the end of it and helped her descend. As he handed her the sack, he cleared his throat, "Well, if I decide to go to the social, will you save a dance for an old goat like me?"

Hannah looked up into his face for an instant and glanced away nervously, "Certainly, Mr. Marston. Thank you for the ride."

"You're welcome, Miss Hannah," he tipped his hat, returned to his buggy and rode away. All the while Hannah berated herself for not assuring him that he wasn't an old goat. The way she'd answered him almost sounded like she'd agreed with him.

Later that evening as the family sat around the dinner table, the conversation turned to the town social coming up on the weekend. As Hannah and her mother discussed the apple and pumpkin pies they'd be baking, Mr. Jamison interjected, "Oh, by the way, Hannah, I was in the mercantile this afternoon and young Mr. Gothard asked me if you were going with anyone to the social. When I told him you had no plans, he asked if he could accompany you.

Since I saw no reason to deny him, I assured him that he could be your escort. He'll be by here around half past six to pick you up."

Mr. Jamison never even looked up to see the aghast expression on his daughter's face, but continued to saw at his pot roast.

"Father! You didn't!" she exclaimed.

"What?" he looked up innocently and shrugged. "Last night you said you weren't going with anyone. You need to start getting out more. You'll be eighteen in April, you know?"

"But Adam Gothard, Father? Please!" Hannah's face grimaced in disgust.

"Yeah, Dad, don't you know Hannah would just as soon go to the fall social with Bubba as that weasel?"

"None of that, Joshua. Adam Gothard is a fine young man – lots of promise in that lad."

"And connections," Joshua quipped sarcastically under his breath.

"As a matter of fact – yes. He does have some fine connections through his father's mercantile." Mr. Jamison agreed. "You could do a lot worse than Adam Gothard."

"She could do a heap better!" Joshua defended his sister.

"That's enough, young man," Mr. Jamison pointed the tip of his knife in his son's direction.

"Please, don't make me go with him, Mama!" Hannah's eyes pled with her mother who simply shrugged in defeat.

"Hannah, you spend the evening with Mr. Gothard, and I'm sure you'll see his fine qualities." Mr. Jamison coaxed.

22

"Uggh!" Hannah rose to her feet, "I can't believe this!" She fled from the table, angry tears brimming in her eyes. If only she'd been flirtatious and convincing enough to have coaxed Ephraim into asking her, she could have told her father that she already had a companion for the evening!

The dreaded Saturday evening came all too swiftly for Hannah. She'd begged and pleaded with both her parents to free her from the distasteful obligation, but neither would relent. When Adam arrived at six-thirty sharp, Joshua sat next to Hannah in her bedroom.

"I think I'm going to be sick," Hannah's hands gripped her stomach.

"That's it! I'll tell Dad you're going to throw up and that you're too sick to go!"

"He'll never believe you," Hannah muttered dejectedly.

"Maybe you can stomach it for one night, Hannah. Just pretend you're dancing with someone else," Joshua attempted to comfort her in vain.

There was a tap at her bedroom door. "Mr. Gothard is here for you, dear," Anna called from the other side.

"I still can't believe they're making me do this," Hannah breathed in frustration as she opened the door and went to her doom.

"Remember dear, look for the good. Look for the good," Anna patted her daughter's shoulder as they went down the hall.

What good? Hannah quipped sarcastically in her own mind as she entered the parlor to find Adam Gothard standing before her in a handsome suit and tie.

He has a nice suit. That's something good. She thought to herself.

When they stepped outside he took her arm and it required every ounce of reserve she could muster to keep from wrenching it away. He helped her into the buggy, *Look for the good – this is a nice buggy, a pretty horse* she told herself as his clammy hands reluctantly released her waist.

Fortunately, he made little conversation on the way to the social and that was something else she could be grateful for – that she didn't have to talk to him. Most of the way, he bit his fingernails and spit them outside the buggy. *At least he's not spitting them at me* she chuckled inside. Humor, yes humor, would get her through the evening.

When they stepped into the town hall, Hannah's eyes scanned the room in hopes of finding some friend to rescue her from the clutches of her tormenter. She smiled at Sarah Townsend and Becky Maples, and they came bubbling toward her.

"Hannah, I just love your dress!" Sarah exclaimed.

"Oh, but I see a small stain right here," Becky pointed to an imaginary smudge. "We're sorry, Mr. Gothard, but we're simply going to have to steal Hannah from you for a moment to take care of this awful stain."

The three girls scurried off, leaving Adam standing in the doorway befuddled.

When they were outside of earshot, Hannah exhaled a deep breath, "Oh, thank you both! I just don't think I could have stood another moment with him."

"At least he's not as wiry and greasy as he used to be, Hannah," Becky tried to comfort her friend. The three sat in a corner and Sarah pretended to rub the imaginary stain from Hannah's dress.

Finally Adam appeared with an outstretched hand, "I can't see a stain there anymore, Miss Hannah. Shall we dance?"

Becky patted Hannah's back consolingly and reluctantly Hannah took Adam's clammy outstretched hand.

Through dance after dance, Hannah listened to Adam rattle on about the new line of tools they'd just got in at the mercantile and how one day all of it would be his – that his father planned to retire in ten years and give him the store. Occasionally he bit a fingernail and spit it aside, or stuck his finger in his ear to extricate some troublesome wax. Hannah counted her blessings that he wiped it on his handkerchief instead of her dress, but nothing could prevent his atrocious breath from nearly gagging her during the slower songs.

About halfway through the evening, during a waltz, Hannah's eyes caught sight of Ephraim Marston's. My, how handsome he was! His hair was neatly combed. The summer sun had lightened it in streaks so that it accentuated his bronze, chiseled features and penetrating eyes. He wore a navy blue suit, and he'd polished his boots to a shine. Hannah couldn't help compare his manly physique to Adam Gothard's pasty-white complexion and wimpy frame. Then her mind shot back to the few times Ephraim had taken her hand. What a contrast from Adam's cold, clammy appendage that required her to periodically dry her hand on her dress between dances!

As Ephraim's eyes caught hers, she tried sending him a message with her thoughts, *Please, Ephraim, rescue me. Just one dance in your arms will make all the torture worthwhile.* As if he could read her thoughts, Ephraim strode boldly across the dance floor and tapped Adam firmly on the shoulder.

"May I cut in?"

Reluctantly, Adam stepped back and released her. Quickly Hannah clutched the folds of her dress to rid herself of Adam's moist residue.

"Thank you," she mumbled as he took her in his arms.

"You looked as if you needed rescuing," his eyes twinkled.

"My parents made me come with him," she whispered. She could feel Ephraim's strong arm pulling her a little closer as if he were assuring her that she was safe for the moment.

"I'm sorry," he whispered in her ear as he pulled her closer still.

"For what?" she asked.

"For –" he hesitated, "that your evening has been so miserable."

"I'm not miserable now," she whispered, and he pulled her back slightly to look down into her eyes. For an instant, Hannah saw something different in the gold and emerald flecks of his eyes, something she'd never seen before. No, she corrected herself. There had been one occasion upon which she'd seen that expression there. It was the day he'd marked the difference between good shivers and bad shivers. With that provocative gaze, she felt the most exhilarating shiver as warmth spread over her starting at her heart and streaming out to her appendages. Then the music stopped, and Adam was back at her side, tapping on Ephraim's shoulder.

"The lady owes me a dance and that last one wasn't a whole song," Ephraim slapped Adam on the back and Adam nearly lost balance from the jovial gesture. "You don't mind, do you, boy?"

Adam reluctantly backed away and gave the couple one more dance.

With that one waltz, Hannah almost came to believe that Ephraim Marston took her seriously – that she was more than a little girl tripping him up and irritating him. With the way he fixed his eyes upon hers and held her in his arms, she felt like a woman for the first time in her life, and a confidence that she'd never known filled her soul. Then, as if a storm brewed within him, Ephraim's expression grew angry. The music stopped and he turned from her, exited the ballroom, and left Hannah standing there wondering what she had done to set him off this time.

She spent the remainder of the evening dancing with Adam, her eyes closed and dreaming of Ephraim instead.

Autumn rolled into winter and Adam Gothard became a weekly fixture at the Jamison household. Hannah's parents invited him for a standing dinner date each Thursday evening and even on Sunday afternoons. Over time, Hannah realized that while the young man's grooming and etiquette were sorely lacking, he could be comical at times and often left the family laughing at his humorous descriptions of people who came into the mercantile.

Still, he wasn't what Hannah wanted in a suitor. He was more like a younger brother who embarrassed you in public and made you laugh at his antics at home. Yet, with each passing day, Hannah feared that her parents wanted something more to develop between the pair. Adam also grew bolder in his advances, taking her hand and touching her arm as he sat next to her. Fortunately, she'd managed to keep him from kissing her.

One gray blustery Sunday afternoon in January, Hannah decided she didn't want to spend another afternoon with Adam and set off for a walk after church. Before long she found herself strolling across Ephraim's pasture to a creek on the other side. She sat down under a tree and wrapped her coat securely around her and drifted off to sleep. Hannah awoke an hour later to thunder cracks. The ground around her was fast becoming a mud puddle. Sheets of rain descended, drenching Hannah's clothing. Through the driving rain she looked around for some place for shelter. She could see the smoke billowing from Ephraim's cabin and headed in that direction. After only a few steps, the rain began to descend so hard that she could hardly see a few feet in front of her. Trusting that she still traveled in the direction of Ephraim's cabin, she battled against the wind and rain. Finally, drenched to the bone and unable to see anything in front of her, she knelt at the base of a tree and called for help. She wasn't sure anyone could hear her over the howling wind, but it was all she could think to do.

She yelled for several minutes and then convinced no one could hear, she slumped to the ground, pulling her hood tightly over her head and prayed for help. A lightning bolt struck the top of the tree she knelt under, and a limb came crashing down, striking her on the back of the head. Within a few moments, Ephraim Marston found her limp body huddled at the base of the oak tree. Quickly he called her name but she did not respond. He lifted her from the earth and carried her back in the direction of his house. The driving rain blustered around him, and he hoped he could find his way back to the cabin.

In the distance he recognized his schnauzer's high-pitched bark, and he battled onward toward the sound of his four-legged friend until he reached his front porch. Quickly he shoved the front door open with his shoulder and carried Hannah inside and laid her on the couch. Boxer, his dog, trotted in behind him still barking excitedly. Ephraim shut the door, bolted it and returned to Hannah's side. Her coat and dress were soaked completely through.

"Miss Jamison," he patted her cheek. "Miss Hannah, wake up."

She didn't stir, so he removed her wet coat and draped it over a chair by the fire.

"Miss Hannah, we need to get you out of these wet clothes," he put his hand to her cheek. Boxer skipped excitedly around Ephraim's ankles as he sat next to Hannah's sleeping body.

"I sure wish you could do this for me, Boxer," he patted the dog affectionately on the head.

Then, with much trepidation, Ephraim removed the heavy wet clothing from Hannah's body, leaving only her undergarments – which really should have been removed as well. But he didn't have the nerve to proceed that far, so he piled layers of blankets on top of her in hopes that they would make up for the dampness of her undergarments. He put another log on the fire and heated the cabin to a temperature at which perspiration dripped from his brow.

He sat in a chair next to her and held her hand in his, gently stroking it. "Hannah, please wake up." She remained so lifeless that periodically he checked her pulse to reassure himself that she still lived.

The wind continued to howl and the rain to fall outside. Fearing that the weather would not let up any time soon, Ephraim went out to the barn to check on his animals and make sure they were all safely enclosed in the structure. While he was gone, Hannah began to stir. Gradually her eyes opened. Her vision blurred at first but cleared shortly and she looked around the cabin, rubbing the lump that had formed on the back of her head. There was a pump at the kitchen sink and a window above it where she could see the rain fiercely descending. A potbelly stove sat in the corner and a round oak kitchen table with two chairs set in the center of the kitchen. In the living room a roaring fire burned in the rock fireplace, and a bear skin rug draped across the hardwood floor next to the couch upon which she lay.

When she sat up, a wave of dizziness hit her and she leaned back on the couch. It was then that she realized that she no longer wore her clothes and a panic seized her. She looked up again toward the fireplace and saw her clothes draped across a chair by the fire. Where was she and why were her dress and cloak removed? She lifted the pile of blankets and discovered that she only wore her undergarments. Quickly she clutched the blankets higher to her chin and her heart leapt into her throat as she saw the doorknob turn and the door fly open. Moisture blew into the room and Ephraim quickly turned and leaned on the door to close it against the violent winds. He bolted it, and Hannah swallowed the nervous lump in her throat.

"Oh, good, you're awake," relief settled in his hazel eyes and Hannah noted how rosy his cheeks were from the cold winds.

She was stunned – uncertain of what to say or do next.

"What in the world were you doing out in this mess, girl?" his voice rose suddenly in irritation.

"I – uh – I went for a walk."

"In the middle of a thunderstorm?" he waved his arm dramatically toward the door.

"It wasn't even raining when I left. I fell asleep under a tree by the creek and when I woke up, it was too bad to make it home. So I saw your house and started this way."

"It's a good thing you did. If Boxer hadn't heard you yelling, you'd have burnt up at the foot of that flaming tree! It's a miracle you weren't struck by lightning. Don't you know to stay away from trees in a thunderstorm?" Ephraim removed his gloves and coat and spread them out before the fire.

"I – I didn't think about that. Thank you for coming after me." She clutched the blankets higher to her chin, suddenly self-conscious, knowing that Ephraim had been the one to disrobe her.

"You need to get out of those wet under things," he suddenly headed toward the back of the cabin. "I'll get you some of my long johns, and you can change into those."

"Oh, I'm sure that's not necessary," she protested nervously.

In a few minutes he returned carrying a pair of white long johns, a pair of trousers, a shirt and a rope. "Here. I'll stay in the back of the house, and you change into these things. Just holler when you're dressed."

Reluctantly, Hannah took the clothing and studied the rope.

"You'll need that for holding up the trousers. I'm a lot thicker in the waist than you are," he explained.

"Oh" she nodded and set the clothes beside her. He left the room.

Anxiously, Hannah changed into Ephraim's clothes. It felt good to be out of her wet things, and she sat before the fire and put on a pair of Ephraim's socks.

"I'm dressed," she called as she looked down at the clothes. She had to roll up the shirtsleeves and the pant legs that made her look like a child dressed up in her daddy's clothing.

"I've got some hot chocolate going," he said as he entered the room and crossed to the kitchen. Amusement filled his eyes as he beheld her drowning in his clothing. "Spread your things out by the fire so they dry out faster."

Nervously she laid out her undergarments on a chair by the fire.

"How are you feeling?" he asked as he ladled two cups of hot chocolate from the pan on the stove into cups.

"My head's throbbing, but I'm well enough," she answered as she took the cup from his extended hand and sipped it slowly. Ephraim moved closer and examined her head.

"You aren't bleeding, but you've got quite a lump there," he noted.

A thunderous crack rattled the house, and Hannah jumped with the jolt of it.

"I'm afraid you're stuck here for a while. That storm's not letting up, and it's already starting to flood the creek and the road. At this rate, we'll be flooded in by morning." He sat down at the kitchen table with his cocoa.

"I can't stay here all night!" Hannah protested.

"Well, you can't get out in that. It's horrible out there," he pointed to the window. "Just go take a look for yourself if you don't believe me."

Hannah crossed to the window and peered out. Lightning danced and thunder rumbled amidst the driving rain.

"Oh, my," she breathed at the sudden realization that she could be trapped in a cabin with Ephraim Marston for days. When the creek around his house flooded, there was no getting in or out of his place until the water receded. "My mother will be beside herself with worry!"

"I know. I'm sorry about that, but there's not much we can do about it," he shrugged. "We'll just have to make the best of it."

At that moment, she wondered if Adam Gothard was stuck at her house, and she became grateful that she wasn't home after all. It would be much better to be trapped with Ephraim and his odd temperament than with Adam and his ever-insistent, repulsive, flirtatious advancements.

She seated herself across from him at the kitchen table. His cheeks were chapped from the wind and the cold. He wore a flannel shirt. The sleeves were rolled up exposing his long johns beneath, and he wore his usual jeans and suspenders. His long legs stretched out on either side of the table. Hannah noted the immensity of his large boots in contrast to her small, socked feet.

"I'm sorry to impose on you in such a manner," she apologized, suddenly realizing that he may be as irritated to be trapped with her as she would have been to be stuck with Adam Gothard.

"You're no imposition," he shook his head assuredly. "Will be nice to have the company. Boxer and I get lonesome around here during the storms."

"I'll try not to be in the way," she offered.

One of his eyebrows rose questioningly.

"I mean I know I get in your way a lot, but I'll do my best not to be a nuisance," she clarified.

Ephraim set his cup down on the table and settled his hands around it to keep them warm, "Miss Hannah, what makes you believe I find you a nuisance?"

Her eyes went up into her head, and she took a deep breath, "Well, let's see here. Shall I innumerate my blunders – first there's the time I spilled punch all over you and then there's the time I let your bull out of the pen and the time I made you drop a fifty-pound feed sack on your foot, and..."

Ephraim raised his hand to stop her. "I've been too hard on you. I've made you think you're a pest."

"And I'm not?"

"No, you're not," he shook his head negatively.

"Then what am I?"

"You're – you're my friend," he smiled.

"Well, thank you, Mr. Marston. That's very kind of you to say," she smiled, grateful that he didn't hate her, yet more than a bit disappointed that he saw her as nothing more than a friend.

With Ephraim's confession of friendship, the awkward tension that usually existed between the pair evaporated, and they spent the evening preparing dinner, eating and Ephraim taught her how to play gin. Hannah caught the knack of it quite quickly, and before the evening was through, she had actually won a round or two.

"It's late. You take my bed, and I'll sleep on the couch," Ephraim offered.

"I couldn't take your room, Mr. Marston. The couch is a perfect fit for me, and you're way too tall to fit on it comfortably."

"You're a lady. And a lady needs her privacy. You take my room, and I'll sleep out here," he insisted.

He took her so off guard by referring to her as a lady, that she became completely tongue-tied and just nodded and headed for the back of the house.

Ephraim followed her. "If you're needin' to get to the outhouse, you better go now. You may have to wade to it in the morning. There's an extra pair of boots at the foot of the bed." He pointed to a large pair of rain boots.

"They might swallow me whole," she chuckled.

"That they may, but yours are still too wet.

She slipped her feet into the boots and tromped down the hallway. Ephraim opened the back door for her, and she stepped out into a sloppy mess of slosh and mud. She carefully stepped through the water that was up to her calves. When she returned to the house, she pulled the boots off and left them by the door. Ephraim bolted the door securely and bid her goodnight.

He'd stoked a fire in the bedroom and added fresh blankets to the bed. Hannah slipped under the covers and pondered on how kind and accommodating Ephraim had turned out to be.

The cracking thunder and howling wind woke Hannah in the middle of the night and she rose from her bed with a blanket draped around her shoulders. She crept down the hall toward the kitchen, hoping there remained a little hot chocolate in the pot on the stove.

As she reached the living room, the flame in the fireplace illuminated the floor before her. She stopped and looked down at Ephraim who lay sprawled out on his stomach on the bearskin rug. He wore no shirt and his hand rested near his face. A blanket draped over his legs, but his bare torso lay exposed. What she wouldn't give to kneel down next to him and caress the locks of his hair and kiss his cheek! Scolding herself for lingering too long to examine him, she ventured onward to the kitchen to get a cup of hot chocolate. There remained only a few sips, but she poured it into a cup and drank.

Ephraim's head shifted from one side to the other, and she stood over him, hoping he wouldn't awake to find her there. Satisfied that he had settled himself, she tiptoed around him. Just as she passed, his arm moved and his hand caught hold of her ankle.

Frightened, she gasped, lost her balance and fell forward, catching herself on her hands and knees. Ephraim leaned on his elbow and rose up lying on his side. He put one arm under Hannah's waist to support her.

"I'm sorry, I'm such a klutz! I was trying to step around you!" she began her apology.

She scrambled to her knees about to stand when Ephraim's hand slid to her cheek and turned her head to look at him. Her pulse quickened and heat rose to her cheeks.

"Stop apologizin', Hannah," he mumbled in his deep smooth voice, and his eyes held that look that she'd only seen on a couple occasions.

"I didn't mean to wake you," she chattered nervously.

"I said to stop apologizin'," he caressed her cheek tenderly and then rose to his feet and helped her to stand. He stood before her in his jeans and bare feet, and she forced herself to divert her eyes from his muscular form. He reached down and lifted her blanket and draped it around her shoulders, wrapping her snuggly within it.

"Get some sleep, Hannah, we'll have a lot of work in the mornin'."

She nodded affirmatively and went back to bed.

Chapter Three

Hannah rose from her warm bed and shivered, even with a blanket draped around her shoulders. She ventured down the hallway into the living room. The fire still blazed, but Ephraim wasn't in the house. The back door was unbolted, so she carefully opened it. The house stood like an island with water surrounding it on all sides. Ephraim's yard had become a lake, but she didn't see him anywhere. She went back inside, set down the blanket, picked up her dress, scarf and coat, which had dried out overnight, and dressed in the bedroom. Pulling the scarf tightly around her ears and neck, she stepped back outside and scanned the area for some sign of Ephraim. She looked toward the barn, which was on higher ground and not flooded by water. Ephraim wore waders up to his chest. He was feeding animals and then lifted two pails of milk.

"Good morning," she greeted.

"Good morning," he nodded.

"Can I help you with anything?" she asked.

He walked toward her, waded through a river of water and handed her the two buckets. "You could make us some breakfast while I take care of the animals."

"All right. I'll do that," she stepped back into the house to find something to cook.

She found some apples in a barrel and made fried apple pies. After stacking a plate full, she put her coat and scarf back on and went outside to let Ephraim know he could come eat. Ephraim bent over, attempting to move some stones to create a pathway to cross to the outhouse. He'd removed his waders since they were hard to work in and tossed them by the back door. With his rear end facing her, she couldn't resist the urge, and put her boot to the seat of his pants and shoved. She didn't think she'd shoved him that hard, but it knocked him off balance, and he fell into the mud on his hands and knees. Hannah threw her hands over her mouth, stunned at her own action and then began to giggle.

She knew she was in trouble and began to back away when he slowly stood erect and turned to face her, mud covering his knees and hands, and a scowl on his handsome face. He clutched a glob of dirt in his fingers and moved toward her.

"Oh, no! Don't!" she pleaded as she backed away from him, still giggling and her heart racing. A sinister smile spread over his lips and his eyes twinkled with mischief. Just as he released the ball of mud, she began to slip on the sloppy ground. The mud splattered on her chest, and she plummeted to the earth, falling on her seat.

"You!" she exclaimed indignantly.

He kept coming toward her, bending down and reaching for another handful of mud as he did so. The mischievous glint in his eyes told her he had no intention of halting his revenge. Nervously, she scrambled backward, unable to reach her feet and scooted away from him, covering the back of her coat with mud and wet grass.

He reared back to throw another gooey clod when she exclaimed, "Please don't! I just came to tell you breakfast is ready!"

"You have a funny way of announcing breakfast," he chuckled and squished the mud between his fingers and teasingly held his muddy hands up as if he planned to wipe them on her dress.

She continued to scoot backwards, clutching at the sloppy muck beside her and flinging it at him with both hands.

He could walk faster than she could scoot, and soon he stood directly in front of her with a muddy outstretched hand.

Thinking it could be a trap, she stared at his dirty hand.

"Truce," he smiled and hesitantly, she put her palm in his. Just as he attempted to pull her to a standing position, they both lost their footing and slipped. He fell directly on top of her, shoving her back into the mud.

"Get off," her hands pushed at his chest and she started to giggle. "You're smashing me." He chuckled and shifted his weight so that he loomed over her, his hands on each side of her face and a knee on either side of her legs.

Hannah couldn't breathe, and it wasn't because he'd knocked the wind out of her. It was from that provocative look which suddenly replaced the mirthful expression. His gaze fell to her lips, and his face lowered to within an inch of hers. Hannah's heart leapt to her throat. Was the man she'd dreamed of for months actually about to kiss her? It appeared as if it were true, until his face infused with anger, and he pulled himself up to his feet and stomped past her into the house, leaving her lying in the mud.

When she entered the house, Ephraim angrily cleaned his hands and arms at the pump. He ripped the filthy shirt from his body and flung it in the sink, followed by his drenched undershirt. In his hurry, he knocked a cup to the floor. It didn't break, but when he went to pick it up, instead of replacing it on the counter, he flung it into the fireplace, shattering it into pieces.

Hannah threw her hands to her mouth. Her astonished gasp alerted Ephraim to her presence. The sheer terror on her face stopped his tirade. His bare chest heaved in and out as his gaze bore into her. Closing his eyes in an effort to control his emotions, Ephraim took a deep breath and exhaled. Water dripped from his face and hair from where he'd rinsed away the mud.

Finally Hannah whispered, "I'm sorry Mr. Marston. If I'd known shoving you like that would vex you so, I never would have done it."

"Would you *please* stop apologizing" he growled through his gritted teeth.

"I'm sorry," she answered, and then threw her hands over her mouth as he bounded toward her. He pulled her muddy hands away from her cheeks and couldn't help from chuckling at the streaks of dirt she'd left there.

"Hannah, please stop apologizing for what's not your fault," his hazel eyes were softer now.

Hannah shook her head as tears welled in her eyes, "I - I'm confused." It was her fault. She'd shoved him in the mud.

"And you have every right to be confused," he released her abruptly and returned to the water pump, dampened a towel and brought it back toward her.

Gently, he wiped the mud from her face and hands.

"You must think I'm a brute," he finally spoke.

"It's just the circumstances – the weather – knowing you're trapped here with someone who annoys you, and you can't be rid of me. I know you were just trying to be nice yesterday. I know you can barely tolerate my presence and here you are stuck with me for who knows how long. It's just the situation."

"It *is* the situation, but it's not what you think," he set the muddy towel on the table and then turned back to her again, his eyes pleading with her for understanding.

"Dear, sweet, Hannah, you don't annoy me." He approached her slowly and she fearfully backed away, tears streaming down her cherry red cheeks.

"Now I've terrified you," he put his hand tenderly to her face.

"Please stop tormenting me, Mr. Marston. I don't know what you want from me."

"What I want from you, I can't have." His thumb caressed her chin. Sadness had now replaced the anger in his eyes.

"I don't understand," she shook her head slightly in confusion.

"I'm not blind, Hannah. I see it in your eyes. What you want from me is the same thing I want from you. But I know it can never be, and then I get angry. I'm infuriated with myself for feeling this way about you and at you for making me feel this way, and then I say or do things that I regret."

"I don't understand."

"Don't deny it, Hannah, I know you lie awake at night wondering what it would be like for me to hold you in my arms, or what it would feel like to have your lips meet mine."

Hannah gasped and reflexively her hand went up to smack his face at the indecency of such a suggestion. He caught her wrist in his hand.

His eyes softened further, "Don't deny it, Hannah. We're past that now. I know what you feel because I feel it myself." He took her hands in his, rubbing them to warm them with the friction of his palms. "We're friends; we can be honest with each other and admit it."

"Are you saying you don't hate me?"

"No, Hannah, I don't hate you."

"Are you saying that you find me..." her voice failed her.

"Adorable, beautiful, irresistible – yes," he finished for her.

Hannah's chest had tightened until she could hardly breathe. He cradled her face in his hands, and he looked at her with such longing that she trembled.

"If you felt that way, why haven't you said anything before now? Why did you allow me to think you hated me?"

"Because I can't have you. I've known that if I dared even once to taste your lips, I might doom myself to a life of knowing what I missed. But right now, Hannah, I think perhaps I will not have truly lived until I've kissed the woman I love."

"You — love me?" she whispered, unable to believe what she'd heard him say.

"Yes, Hannah Jamison, I love you with all my heart and soul. So, what say you? Is it worth the risk of tasting a moment of heaven on earth, even if it can never happen again? Or do we walk away from each other now and spare ourselves the torment of knowing what we can't have?" He released her face and stood with his hands at his sides. "I leave the decision to you, Hannah. You hold my heart in your hands as you have for some time now."

She searched his eyes, not fully comprehending what he was talking about, but she knew if there was any chance she could be held in Ephraim's arms for one brief moment, then she would give everything she had for the opportunity.

With trembling hands, she reached up and put her palm to his cheek and whispered, "I'll risk it."

Not another word exchanged, Ephraim approached her and loosened the knot in her scarf, pulled it gently from her neck and let it fall to the floor. He kissed her cheek gently and his large hands fumbled with the buttons on her muddy coat, opening it down the front.

"What are you doing?" she whispered.

"If this is the only chance I have to hold you, I want to feel you and not your muddy coat," he tossed the garment onto a chair behind them. His strong arm slipped around her back, pulling her against him while his free hand caressed her neck and then her cheek. His mouth lowered gently toward hers, and he sampled the flavor of her lips. Finding them as irresistible as he knew they would be, he gave her the sweet, tantalizing, life-giving affection that Hannah always knew she would receive from Ephraim Marston. Underneath that gruff exterior, she always knew there was a man of passion and even gentleness. Any other man would have struck his mule with a stick instead of patiently tugging on it for an hour.

"Ephraim," she whispered, and with the sound of his name on her lips, both his arms surrounded her, and he kissed her one last time, and held her tightly to his chest. Satisfied that he had embraced her long enough to create a memory to last a lifetime, Ephraim slowly released her and crossed to the fireplace, leaning on the mantel and staring into the flame.

"Ephraim, what's wrong?" Hannah whispered.

"Nothing like this can ever happen between us again," he steeled his emotions, put on his coat, grabbed an apple pie and headed for the door. Just as he reached for the doorknob, Hannah flung herself between him and the door.

"What are you talking about, Ephraim? Why do you keep saying that nothing can ever be between us? If we care for each other this much, why can't there be anything lasting between us?"

He turned and flopped dejectedly in a chair at the kitchen table. "I suppose you may as well know the truth of it all."

She sat opposite him and waited for him to continue.

"I've been to your father four times over the last year asking him for your hand in marriage, but each time he's either put me off or turned me down. He doesn't think I'm right for you."

"I thought you were coming to see my father about a job?" her eyes crinkled in confusion and her heart quickened.

"Yes, the job of being your husband," Ephraim chuckled dejectedly

"Why wouldn't my father give his consent? You're a good, honorable, hardworking man."

"He has someone else in mind for you. Someone he thinks is more suitable."

"Adam Gothard!" Hannah breathed in horror.

"Yep, that's him," Ephraim nodded disgustedly.

"No, I will *never* marry Adam Gothard!" Hannah rose from her chair and began pacing the room. "If you really love me like you say you do, you won't resign me to the likes of Adam Gothard!"

"What would you have me do?" he shrugged his shoulders. "There's no changing your Pa's mind. I've tried."

"But I haven't! When I tell my father that I love you, not Adam Gothard, he'll understand. Surely, he's turned you down because he doesn't know that I care for you. I'll talk with him. You'll see. He'll let us be together."

"And if not?"

"Then promise me, Ephraim. Promise that we'll find a way to be together."

With renewed courage in knowing that Hannah truly cared as much for him as he did for her, Ephraim rose to his feet and took her into his embrace, "I promise. We'll find a way."

Hannah and Ephraim spent the rest of the day cleaning the mud out of their clothes, and caring for the animals. Hannah made dinner for them, and she couldn't help but picture herself cooking every meal in Ephraim's kitchen.

His kitchen became their kitchen, his dog their dog, his house their house. Deep down she felt a comforting reassurance that Ephraim was hers and no matter what happened with her father, they would be together somehow.

Exhausted from a hard day's work, Ephraim collapsed on the couch after dinner while Hannah washed the last of the dishes. She dried her hands on a dishtowel and looked over at him, wishing they were already husband and wife. She approached his sleeping body and gingerly slid onto the couch and put his head on her lap. She stroked the sandy locks of his hair and counted the streaks of gold left from the summer's sun.

She couldn't help but marvel how their relationship had changed overnight. He had gone from a frustrating yet exhilarating puzzle to a man who loved her so much that it drove him to frustration. She could look back now at all those times over the last few years when she thought he hated her and see that what she perceived as annoyance and dislike in his eyes was really his own frustration at knowing he was in love with a woman he couldn't have. Their time alone together had changed everything.

Exhausted, Hannah fell asleep with Ephraim's head on her lap. The next morning she awoke in his bed. Only the side she lay on was disturbed. Ephraim had evidently carried her there and slept on the floor again. She rose and went to the kitchen to prepare breakfast.

Much to Hannah's disappointment, the sun shone and the water had started to recede. Soon she'd have to go home. How would she ever explain to her parents about what had happened?

After lunch, Ephraim sat across the table from Hannah, holding her hand. "It's time I took you home. I think the wagon can make it to your house now."

Her countenance fell, but she nodded affirmatively, realizing that her mother needed to know she was alive and well.

"But let's take a few moments to decide what we should do next," he suggested.

"Do next?"

"Yes, you can't just go home from spending two days alone with me and tell your father you want to marry me. That wouldn't look too good."

"Oh, I see what you mean," Hannah's brow furrowed with concern.

"I don't think there's any hurry to tell your father anything about how we feel about each other. He's not going to let you marry until you're eighteen and that's three more months away."

"So you want me to just keep seeing Adam?" her mouth crumpled in distaste.

"I think it might be best. Of course you don't have to let him get too close," he added with a twinkle in his eye.

She started to protest, and he raised his hand, "Now, let me explain what I'm thinkin' here. I think your father will have a fit if you come back and tell him you're in love with me. He'll think I did something I shouldn't have to confuse you. After all, he does know how I feel about you. So, if we just take you back and act like nothing's changed, and you go about your life as usual, then as it approaches your birthday, we can go to him together and let him know that we both want this. Since you'll be eighteen, he really can't stand in our way at that point. If we have to, we'll elope. But if he finds out now, he could keep us from seeing each other."

"You don't have much faith in my ability to persuade my father, do you?" she stated with a hint of disappointment.

"It's not that I don't have faith in you. I just know your father thinks I'm not good enough for you. Whether you want me or not just doesn't change that."

"All right, we'll do this your way," she nodded. "But I don't know if I can hide the way I feel about you."

"You've hidden it fairly well up until now," he reminded.

"But now it's different. I know you feel the same way. And it's going to be so hard not being able to see you or be with you."

Boxer put his paws on Ephraim's thigh indicating that he wanted to be picked up. Ephraim reached down and lifted the dog, rubbing its head and ears. His hand slipped to Boxer's collar. Suddenly he stood up and carried the dog to the kitchen counter and began fumbling for something.

"What is it?"

"I have an idea," he lifted a little leather pouch, sat back down, removed Boxer's collar and slipped the pouch onto the collar. "We can send messages to each other in Boxer's collar. We'll take him with us today when I take you home so he knows where you live. I'll tell him to find Hannah, and he'll run to you. You tell him to find Ephraim, and he'll carry your messages back to me.

"You think he can really do that?" she chuckled.

"He's a smart little feller; I think I can teach him. We can put messages in there when we want to meet each other or want to tell each other something, and no one will be the wiser," he smiled.

The plan made Hannah feel better. At least she would have some way of contacting Ephraim over the next few months until they could be together all the time.

Ephraim stood up, slipped on his coat, gloves and scarf and assisted Hannah with hers. He readied the wagon and helped her and Boxer into it. Boxer sat on Hannah's lap as Ephraim snuggled her close with his arm around her. They traveled across the wet landscape to Hannah's house. Just before they were to turn onto her road, he stopped the wagon under a clump of trees. He turned to her, the emerald flecks in his eyes even brighter than usual against his wind-chapped cheeks.

"My arms sure are gonna miss holdin' you."

Hannah hugged him tightly, burying her head against his chest. He kissed the top of her head and then gently lifted her chin and kissed her long and hard, the warmth of him leaving her breathless and flushed even though the temperature was almost freezing.

He released her, jiggled the reins and took her home. The moment the wagon reached the house, Joshua, Anna and Harold came out onto the front porch, and Anna Jamison ran to meet them. She barely let Hannah descend before hugging her desperately.

"Oh, we thought the worst had happened!" Anna cried.

"We were so worried!" Joshua exclaimed, and hugged his sister. Mr. Jamison joined into the family embrace as

51

Ephraim looked on, still perched on his wagon, Boxer sitting next to him.

"Where were you? What happened?" Anna felt Hannah's face and arms insuring that she remained unharmed.

"I'm fine, Mama. Mr. Marston found me in the thunderstorm and took care of me."

"He did?" Mr. Jamison's eyes betrayed a hint of anxiety.

"I heard her holler for help and found her. She'd been knocked unconscious by a fallen tree limb."

"Oh, my!" Anna exclaimed.

"He carried me back to his cabin and took care of me. It stormed and then flooded so much that this was the first chance he could get me home."

"Thank you! Thank you, Mr. Marston!" Anna exclaimed, still clutching her daughter as if she might vanish.

"Yes, thank you, Mr. Marston," Harold extended his hand and shook Ephraim's.

"You're welcome. I guess I best be on my way," Ephraim readied to leave.

"Oh, we at least owe you a warming cup of hot chocolate and lunch for your trouble!" Anna exclaimed.

"No, thank you, Ma'am. I'm warm enough," he smiled and nodded. Hannah's eyes darted up to Ephraim, but he did not meet her gaze. "Good afternoon," he tipped his hat toward her parents and was on his way.

Hannah's family hurried her along into the house, and while it should have felt good to be home, Hannah's heart had found a new home with Ephraim.

Chapter Four

A week passed, and Hannah tried her best not to betray the feelings in her heart, but she constantly looked out the window in hopes of seeing Boxer arrive with a message from Ephraim. When the dog never arrived, she began to wonder if the plan would even work. Maybe it was too much to ask of a little dog. Then, Friday morning, when Hannah stepped outside to feed scraps to the chickens, Boxer trotted up the road. Hannah froze. She wanted to run to the schnauzer and quickly retrieve the message from his collar, but she decided against any sudden movement that could frighten him or alert anyone else to her interest in him.

She squatted down and held a biscuit scrap in her outstretched hand.

"Here, boy, want something to eat?"

The dog's pace quickened as he scurried toward her and awkwardly ascended the porch steps with his squatty legs. He snapped up the biscuit and Hannah opened the leather pouch on the collar. Looking quickly around to assure no one observed her, she discretely removed the note from his collar.

Again, she looked around and then opened the strip of paper.

"A stroll by the creek will find me waiting for the one I love."

A smile spread across Hannah's full lips, and her blue eyes twinkled with excitement. Just then, the screen door slammed, and she crumpled the note in her palm and slid it into her apron pocket.

"Hey, isn't that Mr. Marston's dog?" Joshua observed.

"Uh, yes it is," Hannah patted the dog's head with one hand while discretely snapping the leather pouch closed with the other.

"I can take him back home," Joshua offered.

"No," Hannah retorted abruptly. "I mean, I was about to go for a walk anyway. I'll just take him home while I'm out." Hannah lifted the dog and handed Joshua the scrap bucket. "Would you please take that back inside and if Mama asks where I've gone, just tell her I've gone for a walk. I'll be back in a little while."

"All right," Joshua shrugged his shoulders and then took the bucket from her.

Hannah stepped off the porch and started nonchalantly down the road. When she reached the end of the road, she turned right and quickened her pace toward Ephraim's farm. Setting Boxer down so he could trot along beside her, she cut through Ephraim's field and headed toward the creek.

She strolled along the creek for some time, looking for Ephraim and finally found him sitting on a large rock with his fishing line cast into the water. Boxer trotted ahead of her and joined his master. Ephraim pet the animal's head and then looked up to see Hannah coming. She wore her blue dress with her navy coat over the top and a white

54

scarf pulled around her neck. Her curly blond locks
cascaded around her shoulders and her blue eyes stood out
against her rosy cheeks.

Ephraim set his pole on the rock and rose to his feet.
He stood watching her approach, an adoring smile spread
across his lips.

"My, my, Hannah, don't you look prettier than a
butterfly on a spring mornin'!" he stretched out his arms
and she blushed. He stepped toward her and Hannah felt
suddenly awkward and shy. Should she hug him? Kiss him?
How should she greet him? Ephraim answered the question
for her by putting his arms around her and lifting her
slightly off the ground as he kissed her cheek and hugged
her tightly.

His exuberant greeting set her at ease and she hugged
him back, basking in the warmth of his embrace. It felt
good to have his strong arms around her once more.

"Have you missed me, darlin'?" he asked as he put his
hands to her cheeks and drank in her beauty as if it were
the first time he'd ever beheld her loveliness.

She nodded affirmatively, and he lowered his lips to
hers.

Joshua hid behind a large oak tree, his head peeking
around the trunk to observe his sister in an amorous
encounter with their neighbor. In wide-eyed wonderment
he observed the sparks passing between the pair.
Uncomfortable with the lengthy embrace, Joshua almost
stepped from behind the tree to defend his sister's honor
when Boxer did it for him. The dog began to bark at

Ephraim's fishing pole that had just taken off toward the creek.

When Ephraim looked around and saw his pole heading into the water, he leapt sideways, barely grabbing it before it disappeared. He pulled the pole back and quickly reeled in the line to find a large trout on the hook. Hannah put the net under the fish and together they prepared it, cooked it over an open fire and ate their fresh catch on a blanket spread out on the grassy embankment.

Joshua continued to spy in amazement at his sister who seemed so relaxed and enamored with the man who once had been the object of her complaints. Ephraim, who usually acted as if Hannah were a millstone about his neck, now laughed, talked and stared at her as if she were the most beautiful of all God's creations.

When the pair snuggled up at the base of a willow tree, Joshua decided he'd seen enough sparking for one afternoon and snuck off toward home. Rubbing his hands greedily together, his mind set to work thinking of all the goodies Hannah might impart for this information to be kept silent. Oh, he had no intention of really telling his parents about Hannah and Ephraim. He cared for his sister too much for that, but he decided he could get a lot more than a single plug of licorice out of her for this!

Hannah slowly ascended the porch steps, her mind so lost in thoughts of Ephraim and the life they would build together that she didn't notice Joshua sitting on the steps waiting for her.

"You look like you had a good stroll," Joshua noted as she passed him.

"Huh, pardon?" she looked down at his tousled hair.

"I said you look like you had a good stroll," Joshua repeated.

"Oh, yes, it was lovely, just lovely," she continued onward, smiling dreamily.

"Mr. Marston sure caught a whopper today," he added just as she reached for the doorknob.

Hannah halted abruptly, her heart pounding, she froze and then slowly turned to face her brother.

"What did you say?" she asked.

"I said Mr. Marston sure caught a nice fish today for lunch."

Hannah quickly approached her brother and grabbed his arm, pulling him up from the porch and tugged him toward a clump of trees beside the house. Once she felt certain no one would be able to hear them speak, she stopped and put both hands squarely on Joshua's shoulders.

"Joshua Jamison! You've been spying. What exactly did you see?"

"Well, let's see," Joshua rubbed his chin pensively. "I may have seen Ephraim Marston sparkin' with a girl by the creek. I'm startin' to remember who that girl might've been, but I just might forget if I had a good pocketknife to whittle with."

Hannah's eyes widened, "Where would I get a pocketknife?"

"Yes, I believe that girl had curly blonde locks and blue eyes. You know she puts me in the mind of – of you, Hannah!" he retorted with mock astonishment.

"Joshua!" she whispered. "How long were you watching?"

"Long enough to know that Dad would be pullin' out the shotgun if he saw what I saw," Joshua folded his arms resolutely across his chest.

"Oh, you exaggerate. It was nothing so atrocious!" Hannah rolled her eyes.

"It was enough to know you wouldn't want Dad told, would ya?" Joshua issued his threat with his best poker face.

"Where in the world am I supposed to get you a pocketknife?" Hannah whispered, her eyes filled with agitation.

Joshua rubbed his chin again as if he were mulling, "Let's see...Hmmm...I might have an idea... Yes, I saw Ephraim with a mighty fine pocketknife today – you know the one – the one he cleaned that fish with would do nicely."

"You want me to ask Ephraim to give you his pocketknife?" Hannah's eyes widened with anxiety.

"Well, it would be easier on you than the alternative, don't you think?" Joshua bargained.

"You wouldn't tell Dad about it. You're bluffing," Hannah called his threat.

"Do you wanna take that chance?"

Hannah studied his eyes that remained steely. "All right... all right... but I don't know when I'll see him again.

Will you promise to keep your mouth shut long enough for me to talk with Ephraim?"

Joshua put out his right hand, "You've got a deal."

Angrily, Hannah shook his hand and stormed off toward the house.

The next week passed slowly. Joshua kept dropping subtle reminders of the information he possessed - especially when the family gathered around the dinner table. He'd talk about the fish Mr. Marston caught or tease Hannah about the dreamy, faraway look that would periodically catch her eye.

Their parents didn't seem the wiser, but it was enough to remind Hannah that she needed to talk with Ephraim about that pocketknife. When over a week passed with no sign of Boxer, Hannah decided to just go for a walk in hopes she might run into Ephraim.

Thursday evening after dinner, she headed out for an evening stroll. The sunset exploded in the west with a brilliant display of reds, pinks, purples and blue. Hannah ventured past Ephraim's barn and felt someone grab her. She screeched and felt a hand cover her mouth as her back went up against the barn wall.

She ceased her struggle when she looked up into Ephraim's mirthful eyes. Her fear quickly vanished and her pulse quickened with excitement at seeing him standing there before her. He wore a white shirt, rolled up to the elbows, his jeans and suspenders. His left hand leaned against the barn over her head while his right rested at her hip.

"I don't believe I sent for you, woman," he teased in a commanding baritone voice.

"Oh, I can only take a stroll if I'm sent for?" she quipped, a smile twinkling in her eyes.

"No, you take a stroll anytime you like," his head leaned toward hers, and he took her face in his hands. He stared into her eyes, "When you're not with me, I think I remember what you look like. Then when I see you again face-to-face, my heart leaps in astonishment at just how much more beautiful you are than my memory serves."

Hannah looked away sheepishly, embarrassed by his words. But he gently directed her gaze back to him. He took one of her hands and put it to his chest. She could feel the accelerated beat of his heart as he gently kissed her lips, and proved to her that his words were not mere flattery but truth.

"Is that why you came out here this evening, Hannah, to remind me of your beauty and to give me a taste of your sweet lips?" he whispered into her ear as he held her tight against the strength of his body.

Another embarrassed smile flushed her countenance. "Actually, I have a bit of a problem."

He pulled back and studied her somber eyes, "What's wrong?"

"It's my brother," she rolled her eyes. "He saw us out here last week by the creek and now he's threatening to tell my parents unless I give him a pocketknife like yours."

"Oh, is that all?" Ephraim breathed a sigh of relief.

"He can be such a pest. I don't think he'd really tell, but I'd hate to take the chance."

Ephraim pulled his knife from his pocket and held it out to her.

"I don't feel right taking your pocketknife. If I had the money, I'd just go buy him one."

"Nonsense, Hannah, just take it. It's a small price to pay," he jiggled the knife between his fingers motioning for her to take it. When she hesitated, he slipped it into the pocket of her apron.

Hannah threw her arms around Ephraim's neck, kissed his check, thanked him and offered to save up and buy him another one. But he assured her that he had another just like it and it would not be missed.

After only a few moments together, Hannah told him she needed to get home before dark – before anyone missed her. He kissed her one last time, and she slipped away. Ephraim leaned his back against the barn and watched the sun set over the hills. As the full moon and stars made their appearance in the clear sky, he contemplated how perfect it would be to spend a relaxed evening watching the sun set and staring at the stars with Hannah.

Hannah slipped quietly into the house, crept up the stairs and gently knocked on her brother's door. She quietly entered the room and approached his bed. He leaned up on his elbow.

"Before I give it to you, promise me that you'll never breathe a word to anyone about Ephraim and me."

Joshua's eyes lit up in anticipation, gawking at the knife. "I promise, not a word," he nodded.

"Good," she handed it to him and slipped back out of his room, relieved, knowing that while her brother may be a conniving blackmailer, he did always keep his word.

A couple weeks later, Hannah's mother sent her into town for supplies at the mercantile. She breathed a sigh of relief upon discovering that Adam was out on a delivery. While Mr. Gothard gathered the items on the list, Hannah stood at the window watching people walk by. Just as she was about to turn and look around the store, Ephraim caught her eye. Horror of all horrors, a beautiful red head linked her arm through his. It was Rachel Merryweather! She'd left town nearly a year ago, and here she had returned and strolled boldly down the street with Hannah's man!

Anger rose in Hannah's cheeks. Her pulse quickened and her chest constricted. Suddenly the pair stopped and faced one another. Hannah watched in shock as Ephraim leaned his arm against the outside wall of the livery, facing Rachel who stared up into his handsome face. He took her hand in his, looking at it and then continuing to hold it as he carried on his discussion with her. Ephraim released Rachel's hand, smiled at her, tipped his hat and continued on his way alone.

Tears brimming in her eyes, Hannah quickly paid the bill, grabbed her purchases and left the building. She slipped down an alley between the buildings, far enough away so that no one would see and burst into tears. Hannah convinced herself that she had only been a weak replacement, and now that Rachel had returned, Ephraim had chosen her. She should have known it was all too good to be true! Angrily, Hannah took an alternative route home, cutting through fields and berating herself for being so foolish as to ever believe Ephraim Marston would really marry her.

Boxer trotted up the front porch steps and nipped at Hannah's ankles as she sat on the front porch.

"Go away," she shooed the animal. But Boxer continued to pant and prance around her. Finally, more out of curiosity than anything, she opened the pouch and pulled out the slip of paper it contained.

"I hoped to see you in town today. Isn't this shopping day? Sorry I missed you. Please meet me by the barn at sunset."

Hannah rose from the porch, carried the note inside and found a pencil. She scribbled on the back:

"Sorry. I'm busy."

She put it back into the dog's collar and said, "Go home to Ephraim." Boxer trotted away.

The following day, Boxer returned again, *"Hannah, my love, please meet me by the willow at noon."*

"I'm sorry. I can't get away," she wrote her reply.

The next day Boxer returned once more while Hannah sat in the parlor reading. He scratched around on the front door.

"Will you see what that is, Hannah?" Anna called to her daughter.

Hannah grabbed a pencil and slipped out on the front porch.

This time the note read, *"Hannah, my arms are aching for you. Meet me by the creek at lunch."*

Hannah flipped the paper over and scribbled, *"I can't."*

Hannah had been staring at her book for an hour, turning only a page or two the entire time, her mind too occupied with thoughts of Ephraim and how he had turned out to be such a two-timing monster. Again, Boxer scratched at the front door and quickly Hannah slipped outside to retrieve the note.

"Hannah, is there something wrong? Are you all right?" the note read.

"I'm fine," she scribbled and sent the dog on its way.

This time she took her book out on the front porch and waited for his reply.

"Surely you can slip away for a little while. My arms are aching to hold you."

Hannah pulled the pencil from behind her ear and angrily scratched, *"Then, let 'em ache!"*

His reply read: *"Hannah, what's wrong?"*

This time she sent the animal away without an answer.

Boxer didn't return for two more days. This time a silk red rose had been fastened to his collar. He trotted up the porch and scratched on the door.

Joshua opened the door and began to chuckle. He picked up the dog and carried it into the house and up the stairs to Hannah's bedroom. Gently knocking on the door, he said, "Hannah, you have a visitor."

"Who?"

"Let me in and I'll show you."

Hannah slowly opened the door, and Joshua entered carrying Boxer with a silken red rose tied to his collar.

Hannah turned her back to him and flopped down on her bed.

"Don't you want to read the note?"

Hannah quickly turned toward Joshua.

"I know you and Mr. Marston send notes to each other in Boxer's collar," the boy unfastened the silk rose and opened the pouch to remove the note. He put both items on Hannah's lap and sat down with Boxer in the chair across from her.

Hannah stared at both items for a long time until Joshua finally prodded her, "For Pete's sake, Hannah, read the note."

Reluctantly, she opened the paper and read:

"Hannah, I'm sorry if I upset you. I don't know what I did, but I promise never to do it again if you'll just tell me what it was."

Angrily, Hannah retrieved a pencil from her night table and scribbled on the back of the paper:

"Stop playing games with me. You don't have to pretend you still care for me now that Rachel's back."

She determinedly folded the note, put it in the animal's collar, carried him down the stairs and sent him on his way. But, she found that she couldn't throw away rose. She kept it on her nightstand.

That night as Hannah stepped outside after dinner to feed the scraps to the chickens, a strong hand slipped around her mouth and an arm bound her tightly around the waist. She could feel herself being drug off into the darkness. She wiggled and tried to scream, but her muffled sounds were not loud enough for anyone in the house to hear.

Soon she found herself in her father's stable. She stomped at the toe of her assailant and heard him wince in pain.

"Hannah, stop! It's me, Ephraim."

"What's the idea scaring me out o' my skin!" she fussed when he removed his hand from her mouth.

The only light illuminating her face came from the full moon streaming through the hayloft door. But even in that dim light he could see the hurt and anger brimming in her eyes.

"I had to see you. That stupid note writing was getting us nowhere."

"Don't you have someone else to spend your evenings with?"

"What are you talkin' about Hannah? I don't understand all this nonsense about me and Rachel Merryweather."

"Ah!" she pointed her finger accusatorily. "So you admit that there's something going on between you and Rachel!"

"There is nothing going on between us. I don't know where you got that fool notion in your head. The only time I've even seen Miss Merryweather was in town the other day when she was telling me about her engagement."

"See, you *were* with her!" Hannah retorted angrily, and then paused, "Her engagement?"

"Yes, she's home visiting her parents for a few weeks before she marries Luther Madison over in Murfreesboro."

"You mean.. you and she…"

"There's nothing going on between me and anyone other than you."

Hannah flung both hands over her blushing face. "Oh, I'm so sorry! I saw you two together, and you holding her hand and I just thought…"

"You thought I was flirtin' with her, didn't you?" he finished for her.

"It sure looked like it!" she defended herself.

"I was just talking to her, Hannah."

"You sure held her hand long enough!"

"I was looking at her engagement ring. I asked her where Luther got it, 'cause I thought it would be wonderful if I could give you something nice like that."

"Oh," Hannah's hands covered her face once more. "I feel so stupid."

Ephraim chuckled softly and took her wrists in his hands, gently pulling them away from her face.

"You're gorgeous in the moonlight."

"And I'm sure these humiliating tears accentuate my beauty to new heights," she sniffed sarcastically.

Ephraim took her face in his hands and brushed the tears away with his thumb. "I'm sorry, Hannah. I really truly don't have any feelings for Rachel Merryweather."

"But you used to," Hannah sniffed.

"I may have several years ago, but those feelings couldn't hold a candle to the way I feel about you."

"I'm sure it was the way I flung punch all over you both that won you over to my side," she chuckled through her tears.

"Actually, that night was a bit of a defining moment. Whatever feelings I may have had for Rachel disappeared that night."

"Because you didn't like the way she looked in red punch?" Hannah quipped.

"No, because I didn't like the way she treated you. I mean, I know I can be ornery myself at times, but the things she said to you that night were just plain cruel and cutting. I knew I didn't want to be with a woman who had that kind of meanness in her. But you — you stood there and took it without a word of retaliation."

"I ran like a coward."

"You acted like a lady. You never let an ill word escape your lips."

"I ran away like a baby."

"Hannah, she hurt your feelings. I should have had the guts right there, to take you in my arms and let you know that you weren't in the wrong, and that I knew it was just an accident. I'm sorry that I didn't."

"Joshua said you came looking for me."

"I couldn't find you anywhere."

"I went home and cried myself to sleep in my pillow," she rolled her eyes at her child-like behavior.

"But that night – that night was when I realized I had feelings for you. You've held my heart hook, line and sinker ever since, Hannah Jamison. And, you always will."

Hannah threw her arms around Ephraim's waist and buried her head on his broad shoulder. It felt good to be home in Ephraim's arms once more.

Chapter Five

Adam Gothard sat across from Hannah on the front porch. He leaned forward and took her hands in his clammy ones.

"Miss Hannah, we've spent a lot of time together, haven't we?" he began

"Yes, yes we have," Hannah sighed. *Too much time. Entirely too much time!* She thought to herself.

"I've asked your father, and now I'd like to ask you. Would you marry me, Miss Hannah?"

She fought hard to contain the nauseating surge that went up from her stomach and hovered at the base of her throat. Her expression reflexively grimaced in distaste and then she forced herself to control her emotions.

"I can't, Mr. Gothard. You're a nice man, and you'll make someone a fine husband, but I'm not the one for you," she shook her head negatively, and his countenance fell.

"I've rushed you, haven't I?"

"No, Mr. Gothard, you haven't rushed me. You've been a perfect gentleman and if there had been any reciprocal feeling on my part, this would have been plenty of time to wait to ask for my hand. But I just don't feel that way for you, and no amount of time is going to change that."

Hurt filled his eyes and she winced that she had been so blunt.

"Again, I'm sure there are lots of girls who would be interested, but I – I just can't. I'm sorry I've wasted so much of your time. I should have known your intentions and told you sooner."

"But your father assured me that if I asked, you'd accept," Adam defended.

"My father sees what he wants to see. He doesn't see my heart. If he did, I'm sure he would never have allowed you to have your feelings hurt this way. He thinks a lot of you."

Adam nodded dejectedly, rose to his feet, tipped his hat, bid her farewell and left.

Hannah breathed a sigh of relief that the ordeal was finally over and sat out on the front porch looking toward Ephraim's property. "Sweet dreams, my love," she whispered into the air and blew him a kiss.

"Hannah, will you come here for one moment," her father called as she entered the house.

"Yes, Father," she answered and walked back to his study.

"Have a seat," he gestured toward the chair across from his desk and she sat down. "Did Adam ask you anything special tonight?"

"He asked me to marry him, if that's what you mean."

"I was thinking we could have the wedding on June 15th at the church. Then we could hold a reception here at the house. Have you thought about your bride's maids?" Anna queried as she entered the room.

Hannah's incredulous stare turned toward her mother. "I told him no. I have no intention of marrying Adam Gothard!"

"You told him no?" Mr. Jamison's mouth dropped in unbelief.

"What in the world made either of you think I cared for Adam Gothard? Don't you see me recoil from even his simplest touch?"

"Why didn't you say something sooner, dear?" Anna asked as she sat in a chair next to Hannah.

"I did! I told you both before that he repulsed me, but you wouldn't listen. You kept telling me to see the good and kept inviting him over."

"But we thought you had started to like him and could see that he would make an excellent husband," Harold Jamison explained.

"No, I just learned to tolerate him, but there is no way in a million years I could marry him!" The thought of even having to kiss him sent a cold shiver up her spine, causing her to squirm in her seat. "I was just being nice because you wanted me to."

"Oh, dear!" Anna exclaimed.

"What?" Hannah looked at her mother questioningly.

"I've already scheduled the preacher and the chapel. I even had Myrtle start on your wedding dress."

"Just unschedule it and I'm sure one day soon, I'll need that dress. But, I assure you Adam Gothard will not be the groom!"

"And just who do you think you'll marry, Hannah? Who in this little town of ours would make a more suitable husband than Adam Gothard?" her father's voice grew louder.

Hannah rolled her eyes.

He continued, "With Adam you'd have a hope of one day getting out of this flea bitten town; you'd have a nice home and be well cared for. You'd have to search the entire county to find anyone more suitable for marrying!"

"I don't think she'd have to look that far, Dad," Joshua interjected as he leaned on the doorway.

Hannah's wide eyes spun around toward Joshua, shocked that he threatened to betray her secret.

"Joshua," her eyes issued him a stern warning as did her voice.

"Oh, come out with it, Hannah. When are you ever going to find a better time to tell them?"

"Joshua," she muttered, gritting her teeth.

"Tell us what?" Anna asked.

Joshua walked toward Hannah, pulled the pocketknife from his trousers and set it on Hannah's lap. "Hannah's already in love with someone else who will make her a fine husband. He's established, better educated than most folks around here, and he loves Hannah even more than she loves him."

"Joshua, please," Hannah covered her face with her hands.

"What is this nonsense Joshua's talking about, Hannah?" Mr. Jamison's head peered around his son to look at his daughter.

"Tell them, Hannah," Joshua coaxed.

Hannah took a deep breath and then blurted it out, "I'm in love with Ephraim Marston." She released a sigh of relief that the secret had finally been revealed.

"Ephraim Marston!" Harold rose to his feet. "I told that man to leave you alone."

"Why, Father? What's wrong with Ephraim? He's hard working. He's kind and considerate, and he makes me feel valued and loved."

"He's too old for you."

"You're five years older than Mama," Hannah retorted.

"That's different," he quipped.

"How?" Hannah asked.

"He's just a farmer," Harold added.

"You were just a farmer once," Joshua reminded.

"He has no future other than working that land over there that becomes a lake three or four times a year! You'd never step outside of this town if you married him!"

Hannah rose to her feet, "I love him, Father."

"Did he take advantage of you during that storm?" Harold pointed his finger accusatorily and shook his head knowingly.

"He most certainly did not!" Hannah retorted indignantly. "What kind of girl do you think I am?"

"Your father didn't mean it that way, Hannah," Anna answered soothingly.

"Ephraim has never done anything improper toward me!"

"Well, you may not be marrying Adam Gothard, but you're certainly not marrying Ephraim Marston either!" Harold Jamison's jaw clenched resolutely.

"Harold," Anna interjected in a comforting tone. "Maybe this is for the best."

"No," Harold gestured the finality of his decision with a wave of his hand, "No defending her, Anna. I told Marston that he couldn't have Hannah, and my word is final." He pointed his index finger at Hannah, "You aren't to see him again, young lady. If I have to lock you in your room for the rest of your life, you won't be spending time with that no-count farmer!"

"Father, please!" Hannah pleaded, tears now brimming in her eyes. "I don't understand why you dislike him so."

"He's not good enough for you. You deserve better. He's just muddied your mind."

"Father, please!" Hannah pleaded once more but her father only gestured for everyone to leave the room and slammed his study door behind them.

Anna took her daughter comfortingly in her arms and let her cry on her shoulder.

"I'm sorry, Hannah, I never should have said anything," Joshua apologized. "I just thought if he knew how much you loved Ephraim, Dad would understand."

Hannah wanted to yell at her brother but when she looked up to see the sincerity in his eyes, she simply muttered, "It's all right, Joshua. It had to come out sometime." She stepped around him and dejectedly ascended the stairs to her room.

Hannah couldn't sleep. She tossed and turned for hours – angry one moment and in tears the next. Finally, she slipped out of bed, put on her coat and shoes and crept down the stairs and out the back door to the outhouse.

When she emerged, she washed her hands at the pump. Rather than going back into the house, she kept on walking down her road and across the street to Ephraim's farm. The moonlight being all that helped her find her way, she really hoped she wasn't stepping in cow patties.

When she reached Ephraim's dark cabin, she stopped to study the soles of her shoes by the moonlight. Satisfied she hadn't brought along anything disgusting, she stepped onto his porch and knocked on the door.

No answer.

She knocked again.

Something crashed onto the floor inside the cabin and Hannah winced as she heard an angry expletive erupt from Ephraim's lips.

She heard shuffling inside and then a lamplight moved across the window toward the door.

"Who in tar nation," came a growl as the door swung open, and before her stood Ephraim in his long johns, his hair mussed, his eyes squinty, and a grumpy sleepy scowl owning his face.

"I'm sorry, Ephraim, I didn't know what else to do," she apologized.

"Hannah!" his voice softened and a worried expression replaced the scowl. "What's wrong, darlin'?"

"Father found out about us and you were right. He's furious," she sniffed back a tear which threatened to leak from her already tired and swollen eyes.

"Come on in, tell me what happened," he opened the door wider, and she stepped inside. He shut the door, set the lamp on the table and lit another one. "Have a seat. I'll be right back."

Ephraim went down the hall and Hannah sat on the couch, dabbing at her eyes and realizing only at that moment what she must look like.

After a few minutes, Ephraim returned wearing his jeans and a flannel shirt. He sat sideways on the couch facing her.

Hannah let the whole story spill out – all about Adam's proposal and her conversation with her parents afterward.

"He says he'll keep me locked in my room before he lets me see you again," she ended the emotional account.

"Looks like he's not much of a warden – letting his prisoner escape the first night of her incarceration!" Ephraim chuckled.

Hannah giggled lightly and then her expression sobered, "Ephraim, this is serious, what are we going to do?"

"All right.. you're right. We'll figure something out. It's all going to be all right." He patted her knee gently and she put her hand on his. He scooted closer to her and leaned back on the couch holding her hand and thinking.

When he closed his eyes for several minutes, Hannah nudged him with her elbow. "What are you doing? Going to sleep at a time like this?"

"I'm not sleepin'. I'm thinkin'. Give me a minute and I'll have a solution," he answered without opening his eyes.

She waited patiently for another minute and then he opened his eyes and faced her. "I have an idea. You'll be eighteen in a couple weeks – right?"

"Yes,"

"We'll let your father think you're cooperating and then that night, on your birthday, you sneak out of the house just like you did tonight. Meet me out in the middle of the main road, and I'll have the preacher waitin'. We'll get married right then and there."

Hannah's heart began to pound, "Oh, my!"

"What? You have a better idea?"

"No, no, I just," she winced. "My Mama will be so disappointed, and my father will be absolutely livid."

"If you don't want to do it, maybe we could wait and hope some other way comes along," he shrugged.

"No, I want to do it. Let's do it," she smiled, suddenly energized by the idea.

"You sure?"

"Yes, I'm sure. Let's do it. Do you think you can get the preacher to marry us out in the road at night?"

"If I pay him enough, he will," Ephraim assured.

"What time should I meet you?"

"Midnight on the 12th of April."

"Do you mean as the 12th begins or the 12th ends?" she smiled.

"Whichever you prefer."

"Let's get married on my birthday. So at the stroke of midnight as I turn 18, let's get married in the middle of the road," a smile sparkled in her blue eyes.

"Perfect, and if for some reason I can't get the preacher, I'll send you a note with Boxer."

"Better not use Boxer unless you absolutely have to. Joshua already figured out we were sending messages that

77

way. The last thing we need is my parents catching on to it."

"All right," Ephraim suddenly stood, "We'll have no communication between us until that night. Only if there's a hitch in the plan will you hear from me before then."

Ephraim extended his hand and helped her to her feet.

"You better get on home now. I'll walk you as far as your road."

Hannah stood and put her arms around Ephraim's waist, hugging him tightly. He returned her embrace and then reached for his coat.

Ephraim took a lantern and walked Hannah to the start of her road.

"I'm going to miss you," she said as they both stopped and she turned to face him.

He set the lantern at his feet and took her in his arms. "I'm gonna miss you too, but after these two weeks, nobody can ever keep us apart again."

She slipped her hands around his neck and pulled his face toward hers and kissed him like she never had before.

"Hannah, darlin', you better stop that or I'll go for the preacher right this minute," he stepped back and picked up the lantern.

"I love you, Ephraim," she whispered.

He put his hand to her cheek, "I love you, too, Hannah." She watched him until his lantern disappeared over the hill.

Chapter Six

Hannah paced around her bedroom, occasionally pausing to check the clock on her night table. She'd spent the last two weeks sewing a wedding dress. Since her father wouldn't let her go into town anymore, the only material she could find was a white bed sheet. Whenever she wasn't helping around the house, she'd lock herself in her bedroom and sew, all the while thinking of Ephraim and their plans for the future.

Everyone had finally gone to sleep and she looked at the clock that read 11:14. Her stomach churned in a nervous knot and her heart felt like it would literally beat a hole through her chest. What if Ephraim wasn't able to get the preacher? What if her parents heard her slip out of the house? What if he wasn't there waiting for her? Finally she forced the worries from her mind, took a deep breath and reached for her completed dress. Much to her delight, it had turned out very well for being made from a bed sheet! She'd taken some buttons, lace and ribbons from another dress and fortunately she already had plenty of white thread.

She studied herself in the mirror as she arranged her blonde locks with a ribbon and pinched her cheeks for color. Satisfied with her appearance, she turned to the suitcase that lay open on her bed and put a few last items in it and clamped it shut.

She sat down to wait. The minutes crept by slowly. She tried to read a book, but simply stared at the pages. Finally at fifteen minutes until midnight, she extinguished her lamp and carefully left her room, quietly descended the stairs, placed a brief note about her elopement on the kitchen table and slipped out the front door.

Hannah could literally hear the thumping of her heart in her ears as she traveled down the road carrying her suitcase. Every few steps, she'd turn and look back to the house to make sure no one had observed her leaving.

When she reached the main road, she checked to her left and to her right, but all was blackness. No preacher. No Ephraim. Her throat began to tighten. Where was he? Had he sent a message and she never got it? She decided to walk toward Ephraim's house, but just as she turned to her right, she caught a flicker of light coming from the opposite direction. She turned toward town and there came Ephraim driving his wagon with the preacher sitting beside him holding a lantern.

Hannah hurried toward them, and Ephraim stopped the wagon in the middle of the road and hopped down to meet her.

"Hannah, you look beautiful," he smiled.

She threw her arms around him and hugged him tightly, so relieved was she to see him there.

"You look so handsome!" she adjusted the lapel of his navy suit and kissed his cheek.

Two men hopped off the back of the wagon.

"The most clandestine wedding I ever did witness," Ephraim's friend Gavin chuckled.

"I'll say," added Gavin's brother Gordon as he spit a wad of tobacco into the grass.

The preacher cleared his throat to get their attention. Ephraim took Hannah's hand, and they stepped in front of the preacher. Gordon and Gavin took their spots on either side of the couple. The old gray-haired balding gentleman held the lantern up in his long slender fingers while he held his book in his other hand.

"Dearly beloved, we are gathered here this day – er – I mean, this night to join this man and this woman in holy matrimony," the preacher continued through the ceremony in a business-like manner.

Upon pronouncing them man and wife, the couple kissed and Ephraim lifted Hannah and her suitcase up into the wagon and climbed in next to her. The preacher took his seat next to Hannah while Gordon and Gavin hopped in the back of the wagon.

Ephraim turned the loaded wagon around and headed back toward town. They stopped in front of the preacher's house and after the newlyweds had thanked him properly, they proceeded onward and dropped off Gordon and Gavin at the livery.

"Thanks, fellas!"

"Congratulations, you two!" Gavin waved.

"Enjoy your trip!" Gordon added.

"Trip?" Hannah inquired. Ephraim just put his arm around his bride and pulled her close.

"It's kind of chilly. There's a blanket down here," he mumbled and pulled a blanket from the wagon floor and draped it over their laps.

When Ephraim didn't turn the wagon back toward his house, Hannah asked again, "Where are we going?"

"It's a surprise; get some sleep," he pulled her close and she nuzzled into his shoulder, content and relaxed for the first time in weeks.

A few hours later, Ephraim pulled the wagon in front of a hotel. As he shifted from the seat, his movement awakened Hannah. She sat up and looked at Ephraim and then toward the building.

"Where are we?" she yawned sleepily.

"Nashville," he smiled.

"Really? I've always wanted to visit Nashville!" she looked around in wide-eyed wonderment. She couldn't tell much because it was still so dark outside.

Ephraim set their suitcases on the sidewalk and helped Hannah from the wagon. He shifted his own bag under his arm, lifted Hannah's and then extended his free arm to her.

Once inside, Hannah's eyes traveled the interior of the grand hotel. She had never seen such ornate woodwork or elegant chandeliers, carpet and draperies.

Ephraim paid the clerk and a bellboy led them up a cherry spiral staircase to the second floor. They walked down the plush burgundy carpeted hallway that overlooked the spacious foyer. The bellboy unlocked the door, set the luggage inside the room and returned to the doorway to hand Ephraim the key. After tipping the bellboy, Ephraim turned to Hannah and without a word, scooped her up in his strong arms, carried her over the threshold, into the room and shut the door.

As dawn broke over the Tennessee hills, the morning's rays streamed softly through the window on the sleeping couple. The light fell directly in Hannah's eyes, and she awakened to the face of her resting husband. If she hadn't felt the cool spring morning chill on her shoulders, she would have sworn the entire thing had been a dream. She watched him sleep for some time and then gave in to the irresistible urge to assure herself that she truly had married Ephraim the night before. She gently stretched out her hand and brushed a lock of his hair from his eyes and felt the morning bristles on his cheek.

Ephraim's eyelids fluttered at her touch. When the emerald flecks of his eyes gazed back at her, Hannah smiled.

"Good morning, sleepyhead," she greeted.

"Good mornin', beautiful," he traced the contours of her face with his fingertips.

A wide grin suddenly spread across Hannah's full lips.

"What are you smiling about?" he asked.

"To think my father said if I married you I'd never set foot out of town. Here we are, married only a few hours, and I've already been farther away from home than I've ever been before!"

"This is nothin', darlin'. Nashville's just the closest place to catch a train."

"You mean there's more?" Hannah's eyes widened expectantly.

Ephraim's face lit with excitement as he leaned on his elbow facing her, "Where do you want to go, Hannah? Wanna see Boston? New York? The nation's capital?"

"It all sounds wonderful," Hannah answered dreamily and then added. "You're talking about some day - right? You're not talking about now, are you?"

"Not this minute, but after we see Nashville, we'll go wherever you want to go next - we'll see it all."

"Really?"

"I've been saving up a long time for this. Gordon and Gavin have agreed to watch the farm while we're gone - a whole month if need be."

Hannah excitedly threw her arms around his neck and kissed him. "I never dreamed, Ephraim! Just being with you was all I wanted. I never imagined you'd surprise me with something like this!"

"I love you, Hannah. I want to see your eyes light up like this every morning of my life."

"They will as long as I wake up next to you."

~*~

Ephraim was true to his word; they caught a train and took a tour of the northeast. They visited the sights of the nation's capital, took in a Broadway play in New York City, and ate clam chowder in a café overlooking the Boston Harbor. After a full month of travel, they arrived back at their little cabin, travel-worn but full of lasting memories.

When they entered the cabin, Gavin greeted them, "Well, well, well, thought you two lovebirds were never gonna return. Did you have a good trip?"

"It was wonderful! Simply wonderful!" Hannah hugged her husband's arm.

"Everything all right while we were gone?" Ephraim asked.

"The crops are coming in nicely. The animals have all been fine, as you can tell Boxer's missed ya," Gavin pointed at the little dog that nipped excitedly around Ephraim's ankles. Ephraim reached down and lifted the dog turning his cheek when it happily licked his face.

"What about my family? I sent them some postcards. Have you heard from them?" Hannah asked.

"Mayor was fit to be tied. Came over here that mornin' after y'all left – just a rantin' and a railin – demandin' I tell him where y'all went. Course I didn't know... so I couldn't tell him."

Hannah winced, gritting her teeth knowing full well the breadth of her father's fury.

"He sent young Joshua over here a couple weeks ago with this letter for ya," Gavin pointed to an envelope on the table.

With trembling hands, Hannah reached for the envelope and broke the seal. Ephraim stood behind her, putting his arms comfortingly around her waist offering her strength for whatever she might find inside.

She pulled the paper out and read:

Mrs. Marston,

This letter is to inform you that from this time forth, you are no longer a part of the Jamison family nor are you welcome in our home. You have trampled upon the wishes of your parents, have run off like a trollop and disgraced our family's good name. Do not attempt to contact any member of this family in any way. Neither you nor your low-life husband are welcome on our premises or in our lives.

Sincerely,

Mayor Harold Jamison

Hot tears welled in Hannah's eyes and an angry, hurtful lump caught in her throat.

"It's gonna be all right, Hannah," Ephraim's deep voice offered consolingly as she turned to him and released her tears into his sturdy shoulder. He patted her head and held her tight, letting her cry.

"Time will heal it, darlin'," he added.

Hannah started to reply that her father was the most hardheaded man she knew and that she doubted he'd ever soften, but the tears choked the words. She just held onto Ephraim all the tighter. He was her world now, and he'd proven to her that a world with him was a lot bigger than she ever dreamed it could be under Harold Jamison's roof.

The thought gave her strength and she pulled her handkerchief from her apron, dried her tears and stoically entered the kitchen, "If that's the way he wants it, that's the way it will be. This is my life now – here with you. And I'm happy to make the best of it." She forced a smile and set to work making lunch for her husband.

As they ate, Ephraim suggested that Hannah use Boxer to send her family a note. After all, she knew Joshua would want to hear from her and most likely her mother would too. It was only her father who had shut her out of his life. Hesitantly, she swallowed her pride and agreed. She slipped the note inside Boxer's collar and sent him on his way:

"Joshua, I'm home. We had a wonderful trip. If father didn't let you see the postcards, we visited Boston, New York and DC. Missing you! Send Mama my love. - Hannah"

A short while later, Boxer returned with:

"I'm so happy for you Hannah! Sure am missing you. Will sneak over when I can. Mama misses you, wants to visit, but he won't let her. Hope you don't mind, I told her about Boxer. Love, Joshua."

And another slip enclosed read:

"Hannah, sweetheart! I've missed you so! While I wasn't pleased with your elopement, I can understand why you did it. I'm glad you're happy. I want to see you! I may have to sneak out with Joshua! Love always, Mama.

"See there, darlin', I told you that you should send that note," Ephraim hugged his wife as bittersweet tears brimmed in her blue eyes.

"You're always right. When will I ever learn that?" she chuckled.

"I don't know. When will ya?" he teased.

Over the next few months, Hannah continued to communicate with her brother and mother through Boxer. Mr. Jamison, smelling mutiny among his family members, kept a strict eye on them, making it impossible to sneak away. He even deliberately took them to a different church so they couldn't catch a glimpse of Hannah across the congregation. Upon noting his wife's unusual jovial countenance after shopping in town one afternoon, he started dropping off the shopping list himself and had the items delivered directly to the house.

Anna and Joshua began to feel like prisoners in their own home and the pressure in the household began to escalate like an old rickety boiler ready to explode.

"Frank Allen told me at the last town council meeting that ignorant old Ephraim Marston thinks he can reroute the creek so that it won't flood his property," Harold sneered over dinner one August evening.

"It sure would be nice if he could find a way to control the waters," Anna answered.

"Humph! More likely he'll mess up somethin' else – cause our house to flood or someone else's in the process!" Harold retorted angrily.

"I heard he had an engineer come out and help him decide what to do," Joshua added. Anna sent her son a discreet silencing expression.

"Where did you hear that? Have you been over there talking to them?" Harold exploded.

"No, no. Just one of my friends stopped by and told me." Joshua wondered when his father thought he'd been out of his sight long enough to step off the property.

"Engineer or no. I'm going to put a stop to it." Harold thumped his fist on the kitchen table, rattling the dinner dishes.

"What are you going to do?" Anna asked worriedly.

"I'm the mayor of this town. I'll see to it that tonight the town council puts a stop to this nonsense before Marston messes up the entire area tinkering around with that creek!" Harold determinedly rose from his chair and prepared to leave for his council meeting.

When he stepped out of the room, Joshua whispered to his mother, "We've gotta warn Ephraim."

"I know, I know..." she whispered.

When Harold left the house, he turned back with a stern warning, "You two stay put tonight, ya here!"

"Where would we go?" Anna shrugged her shoulders. She watched Harold ride away and then turned to Joshua, "Take the lantern and go over and let Hannah and Ephraim know what's happening. Ephraim needs to be at that council meeting tonight."

"Yes, ma'am," he nodded, grabbed a lantern and left.

Joshua pounded on the front door of the cabin. Ephraim opened the door and happily pulled Joshua inside, "Hannah, you have a visitor!"

Hannah couldn't believe her eyes when she beheld her brother standing just inside the door. They embraced each other, and she carried on about how much he'd grown since she'd last seen him in April. When she started to ask about how her mother was, Joshua interrupted the long-overdue exchange of greetings and got to the point.

"We don't have time. Dad's at the town council meeting tonight, and he's proposing a plan to stop Ephraim from diverting the creek." He turned to his brother-in-law, "You need to get down there and defend your plan. Take your engineer if you can."

Ephraim grabbed his coat and hat, "Do you want a ride home?"

Joshua looked to his sister.

"Won't you stay here a while?" she pleaded.

"I can't. If he finds out I snuck out to warn you, I'll be in for it."

Hannah nodded with understanding, hugged her brother one last time and kissed her husband before Ephraim and Joshua left the cabin together.

Ephraim burst in the back door of the town hall. Mayor Jamison and six council members sat around an oval table. Jamison had just raised the issue of Ephraim's plans regarding the creek.

"I believe I have a right to state my case before you summarily rule on what I can or cannot do with my land," Ephraim towered over Jamison, his fist clenched at his hip.

"Marston, what are you doing here?" the Mayor's eyes raked over Ephraim from head to toe as if he were looking at a smelly pile of horse manure suddenly dropped from the ceiling onto the floor in front of him.

"Protectin' my right to do what I please with my own land!" Ephraim retorted.

"It's not your land you're foolin' with here. You're diverting a creek that crosses a lot of other people's property and when you go foolin' with it, you're going to wreak havoc on other people's property!" Jamison rose to his feet, his short stocky body holding no intimidation against Ephraim's towering form.

"First of all, you've got the story all messed up. I'm not diverting the creek," Ephraim answered.

"What exactly are you doing, Mr. Marston?" Jack Mulberry, a soft-spoken, councilman inquired.

"I've had an engineer come out and take a look at it. He says if I dig a pond on my land in a specific spot and put in some trenches from the creek to that pond, then when it overflows, it'll go into the pond and not my entire property."

"Sounds like diverting the creek to me! You'll be stealing the water the rest of us need and hoarding it into a pond on your property!" Jamison roared.

"No, the trenches will be at a higher elevation so that when the creek is normal, it won't ever spill into the trenches. The only time the creek water will get into the trenches and make its way into the pond will be during those three or four times each year when the creek overflows. All I'm doing is keeping it from running all over my property and keeping it localized in one area."

"And the engineer thinks it will work?" Jack Mulberry queried calmly.

"Yes, he does. He's marked all the spots for exactly where I need to dig and where I need to place the trenches." Ephraim handed Mr. Mulberry a set of plans for the project and the men gathered around to examine it for some time.

"Looks good to me," one man commented.

"But what if he's wrong? What if it doesn't work?" Harold Jamison demanded.

"Then, I'm the only one that's hurt – I'm the one who will have wasted all the effort diggin' around on my property." Ephraim replied.

"Is there a possibility that what you're doing could harm anyone else?" another councilman asked.

"No, sir, not a chance. The engineer assured me of that."

"Then I see no reason to stop you from doing it," Jack Mulberry rolled up the plans and handed them back to Ephraim.

"Come on, now, men! Can't you see this is a crock of nonsense?" Jamison turned his angry eyes back to his associates.

"Perhaps we should take a vote," Jack suggested.

"I second the motion," another man agreed.

"Who thinks Mr. Marston should be allowed to attempt to control the flood waters on his land?" Jack raised his own hand and everyone but Harold Jamison raised theirs.

"All opposed," Jack continued. Jamison angrily lifted his hand.

"Looks like you can do as you please, Mr. Marston, given you stay within the engineer's proposed plan," Jack stood and extended his hand to Ephraim who shook it firmly.

"Thank you," Ephraim said and then thanked the other men who had approved of his plan. Jamison remained standing, glaring at Ephraim as he left the room and quietly shut the door.

Jack put his hand on Jamison's shoulder and gently explained, "Mayor, it is the duty of men in our position to put our petty differences aside and do what is just and honorable."

Harold glared at Jack and then calmly took his seat and continued the meeting, "What's the next item of business?"

~*~

Anna carried her basket of wet laundry outside and set it on the grass. A gentle wind blew as she retrieved a clothespin from her apron and fastened one of Joshua's shirts to the clothesline. As she reached for another garment, she spotted Boxer trotting across the lawn. She quickly hung up the next item and beckoned the dog to join her by tapping her hands on her knees and calling his name.

She patted the dog's head and removed the note from his collar.

"Ready to be a grandmother? How does March sound?

I love you!

Hannah"

"A grandmother! I'm going to be a grandmother!" Anna exclaimed, clasping her hands for joy. Excitedly, she lifted her skirt and scurried toward the house in search of Joshua.

~*~

Upon starting the task of digging the trenches and the pond, Ephraim discovered that it was more than one man could handle. With Hannah nauseated most of the time, she couldn't help. So working on a budget, Ephraim hired a few men to help him with the pond, and his friends Gavin and Gordon donated what time they could on the weekends.

One September morning, Ephraim worked alone out by the creek, digging the trench that would carry the overflowing water to the pond. It had been raining so it made a muddy job. He stood inside the trench facing the creek, digging. Ephraim inserted his shovel, and just as he tossed the dirt aside, the muddy ground gave way beneath his feet and he fell, sliding into the creek. As his feet landed in the water, his head fell back on the embankment striking a creek rock.

When he didn't return for lunch, Hannah decided to carry it out to him. She rounded up a picnic basket and set off with Boxer to the creek to relieve her husband from a hard morning's labor. When she reached the creek, she didn't see him and began calling his name. No answer came.

Hannah carefully examined the trench Ephraim had been digging. Noting that he hadn't made much progress since the day before, an ominous sensation spread over her. With trepidation she ventured closer to the creek and caught a glimpse of Ephraim's legs dangling in the water. His body lay limp on the rocks and blood caked on his face and hair.

"Oh, my! Ephraim!" she flung her hand to her chest in shock. "Ephraim! Ephraim, wake up!" she called, looking down at him, unsure of what to do. Boxer had joined her and barked as he too peered over the edge at his master.

After a momentary battle with confusion and panic, Hannah quickly pulled her shopping list from her apron, tore off a piece, and set the paper on a rock and wrote,

"Ephraim's been hurt by the creek. Please get a doctor, fast! And bring some extra men to help. He's fallen in the creek." – Hannah"

With trembling hands she put it inside Boxer's collar and sent him for Joshua, all the while praying for her husband and hoping the doctor would arrive quickly. She knew she needed to reach Ephraim, so carefully she sat down on the embankment and eased herself down onto the rocks next to him. Gently, she lifted his head and shifted herself under him so that his wounded head would rest on her lap.

Putting a palm to his chest, she could feel him breathing and his heart beating. She dampened her handkerchief in the water and began cleaning his head and examining the wound.

"Ephraim, wake up, it's me, Hannah," tears drizzled down her cheeks. "You're going to be ok. I sent Boxer for Joshua. He'll get the doctor. Everything's going to be all right." All she could do now was pray and wait. It seemed like hours, but really it was only about twenty minutes before she heard her mother calling her name.

"Mama? We're over here! In the creek by the trench!" When she looked up to see Anna's worried face, she asked, "Did you send Joshua for the doctor?"

"Yes, he's on his way. How is he?" Anna asked.

"He's breathing, and I can feel his heartbeat, but he won't wake up."

"Just stay down there with him and keep him still until the doctor arrives."

Hannah's anxiety lessoned now that her mother was with her. So comforting to her was Anna's presence that she even took a moment to say a prayer of thanks to God for sending her.

Ephraim being no small man, it took the doctor, Gordon and Gavin to lift him from the creek on a stretcher. They did their own slipping and sliding during the task, and Hannah held her breath praying they would be able to lift him out without causing more damage to his wounded body.

Loading him on the back of the wagon, they drove him back to the house with Hannah next to him, continuing to talk to him, hoping any minute that he would awaken. When they reached the cabin, the men carried him into the house, and helped Hannah remove his muddy clothes and put him into bed. The doctor bandaged his head and examined him for further injuries.

"He doesn't appear to have any broken bones. His neck is all right. He's got quite a concussion, and we're just going to have to wait and see if he wakes up."

"If he wakes up?" Hannah exclaimed and her mother tightened her arm around Hannah's shoulders.

"I'm sorry, Mrs. Marston, but there's a chance he might not wake up. But many times people do wake up and are just fine after something like this."

Hannah sat on the bed next to her husband, leaned over and rested her head on his chest. She could feel his rhythmic breathing, assuring her that he still lived. He would be fine. Yes, he had to be, she told herself. The others slipped from the room, giving Hannah time to be alone with her husband.

Hannah never left Ephraim's side. Her mother and Joshua went home, but then returned to bring her dinner. The doctor also left, but stopped by every few hours to check on Ephraim.

In those lonely hours, she talked with him about their plans for the future, about the baby and what a wonderful father he would be. She read to him from one of their favorite books and even let him win a game of cards.

That night, she crawled in bed next to him, draped her arm over his chest and pretended that he was just sleeping and that in the morning he'd wake up like every other morning, kiss her, milk the cows and feed the animals. Hannah worried more than she slept, and it was nearly four in the morning before her exhausted mind and body finally gave up the fight and drifted off to sleep.

Chapter Seven

Hannah dreamed that she and Ephraim were standing in front of the Statue of Liberty, just like they had on their visit to New York. Ephraim pulled her close. She could feel his strong arms around her and the warmth of his lips to hers. She could feel her fingertips lost in the thick softness of his hair. It seemed so soothing and real that she opened her eyes to find that indeed it was. Ephraim lay next to her, kissing her awake.

"Wake up, sleeping beauty," he smiled.

"Ephraim!" she exclaimed and bolted upright, "You're awake!"

He gently put his palm to the bandaged lump on his head, "What happened?"

"Don't you remember?"

"The last thing I remember was eating breakfast, milking the cows and walking toward the creek."

"You were digging the trench and you must have slipped. I found you with your feet in the creek and the rest of you lying on the rocks. The doctor says you have a concussion."

"How did you get me out of there?"

"I sent Boxer to Joshua with orders to get the doctor. Then the doctor and Gavin and Gordon came to help get you out. Even Joshua and Mama came!"

"You mean your father let them out of his sight?" his eyes widened with amazement.

"I don't think they asked permission," Hannah chuckled. "How do you feel?"

"Achy. Hungry."

Hannah leapt from the bed to make breakfast, but then a wave of nausea hit her. She stopped to hold her stomach and regain her composure.

"Are you all right?"

"Oh, just the usual," she smiled weakly and continued toward the kitchen.

Just as Hannah prepared a plate of food for Ephraim, he emerged from the bedroom dressed in his work clothes. Still light headed, he tried to reach the kitchen table before Hannah saw him staggering about.

"What are you doing up?" she asked. "Get back to bed right now!"

"I'm fine. There's work to be done." He pulled out a chair and with great internal relief, sat down.

"Nonsense! You can't work. I'll take care of things around here." She set the plate in front of him and then sat beside him with her own breakfast. Ephraim let the matter drop for a moment, unwilling to waste his energy on an argument. After breakfast, he rose from the table and helped Hannah clear the dishes.

"I told you to go back to bed. Stop helping me," she scolded. He turned as if he were going back to bed and then circled around the table to the front door and opened it. Just as he started to step outside, he met the doctor with his knuckles raised to rap on the door.

"You're awake!" the doctor exclaimed, letting his hand drop to his side.

"Yes, I'm feeling just fine now," Ephraim thumped his chest to indicate his spry condition.

The doctor looked Ephraim up and down, "Why are you dressed in your work clothes?"

"Got cows to milk and a pond to dig."

"Oh, no, you don't," the doctor pushed Ephraim back inside the house, grabbed his arm and started leading him back to bed.

"I can't lie in bed all day. I've got work to do," Ephraim protested. Hannah watched the entire exchange with a smile, happy that she had reinforcement.

Just as the doctor led Ephraim down the hall, Gavin peeked his head in the door, "Mrs. Marston, I'm going to go milk your cows. Would you please give me a couple milk pails?"

"Thank you, Gavin! That's so kind of you!" Hannah reached for the pails and handed them to Gavin who tipped his hat and set to work.

As Ephraim's head hit the pillow, he had to admit to himself that he was in no state to be milking cows, much less digging a hole.

"I don't want you doing anything strenuous for at least three or four more days," the doctor ordered.

"What?" Ephraim raised up on his elbows to argue, but the doctor just pushed against his chest sending him back on his pillow.

"No arguments. I'll see that you and the Mrs. have help around here."

Tired, aching and his head pounding, Ephraim decided he'd save his energy to fight later. Before long, he'd drifted off to sleep.

Several days later, Ephraim and Hannah milked the cows, and Ephraim set out with a shovel to start working on the pond again. He'd lost an entire sunny week and from the clouds in the distance, he knew the rains were coming. Once it started raining, digging a pond would be next to impossible.

Much to his surprise when he reached the pond, he found that it was nearly completed, and he'd barely made a dent in the project before the accident. Just as he surveyed the amazing progress, two wagons full of men approached – one driven by Gavin and the other by Gordon.

They stopped the wagons and the men poured out, carrying picks and shovels. They immediately set to work and Gavin and Gordon joined Ephraim, greeting him with handshakes.

"You two did all this?" Ephraim marveled, choking back a lump that had formed in his throat.

Gavin waved his arm toward the men, "We had quite a bit of help."

"I don't know what to say," Ephraim shook his head amazed that his neighbors would do so much for him.

"How about thanks?" Gordon teased.

"Of course, thank you!" He raised his voice so all could here, "Thank you all so much! It doesn't seem like enough to just say thank you."

"Ah, if it had been one of us, you'd have done the same thing," Gavin noted.

"I hope I would have," he remarked to himself as he moved closer to the pond and set to work.

~*~

Hannah sat across from Ephraim at the kitchen table. The baby kicked and she reflexively put her hand to the spot as Ephraim tossed four aces onto the table.

"Let's see ya beat that!" he grinned triumphantly.

"You've got me there," she laid her cards face down and awkwardly rose from her chair. With the baby due in only two more months, her large stomach caused her to waddle slightly. She crossed to the window and peered out. "It's really coming down out there. You think the pond will hold it all?"

Ephraim joined her at the window, "Hope so...sure hope so."

"I, for one, will be glad when it stops all this raining. It's so dreary and monotonous."

"On the bright side, it'll be a good test. If it can hold this much water, we'll know it can withstand just about anything. Then we'll know that there will be no problem planting all the land in the spring."

"That's true. I'll keep trying to look at the bright side." Hannah turned and embraced her husband.

When the baby kicked, Ephraim put his hand to her abdomen, "I think someone else wants to get out and see the sunshine. We think we've got it bad. I'd hate to be cooped up in that little place."

"Yes, I guess you're right about that!" Hannah chuckled.

The next morning, the rain had stopped and Ephraim rose early to check on the pond. Hannah waited expectantly in the kitchen for his return.

"So far, so good," he smiled as he stomped into the house and pulled off his boots, leaving them by the door. "Of course, it'll continue to rise throughout the day, but by afternoon we should know."

"Does it look like it'll hold?"

"Looks promising. No way to be certain yet. We'll just have to wait and see."

Ephraim and Hannah spent the day working and periodically checking on the pond. As they stood together looking at the brimming receptacle of the floodwaters, Joshua joined them.

"Looks like you did it, Ephraim!" Joshua exclaimed and slapped his brother-in-law on the back.

"Yep, with the town's help, we did it."

"No thanks to Dad!" Joshua interjected with a disgusted roll of his eyes.

"Ah, don't be so hard on your Pa," Ephraim put an arm around Joshua. "I guess I'd be mighty sore too if someone stole somethin' this beautiful from me." He lifted Hannah's hand to his lips and kissed it.

"But you didn't steal her. She's right here in his backyard, and he won't swallow his durn pride to even come see her."

"At least he's letting you and Mama visit occasionally. He's softened quite a bit," Hannah noted.

Joshua nodded affirmatively, but he didn't want to let Hannah know just how much flack his father gave them both each time they returned from a visit to the Marston's.

~*~

The March winds whipped Hannah's curls into her face and she wrestled with them, trying to keep them inside her bonnet. Ephraim had plowed the field and left her to plant the seeds while he moved on to plow another field. Normally she enjoyed planting season, but this year, with her stomach bulging, she could hardly stand to bend over. When she managed it for more than ten minutes at a time, nature would call her to the outhouse.

Hannah stood back looking at the row. Just a few more feet and she'd have all the beans in. She planted four more and then doubled over with pain and fell on her knees. When the wave passed, she awkwardly pulled herself to her feet and wobbled toward the front porch. She rang the bell on the front porch, signaling Ephraim to return. Another contraction hit and she leaned on the doorpost, bracing herself against the pain. When it subsided, she rang the bell longer and louder and then went inside the house to sit down.

"Is it time?" Ephraim burst through the front door and flung his hat on the table. He immediately knelt next to Hannah who had put her feet up on the couch.

"I think it is," she nodded breathlessly.

He gently brushed the hair from her face and then took her hand. Her grip tightened on his and her breathing became erratic. "Go ... " she panted. "Go get ...my mother."

"I should send for the doctor," Ephraim stood, still holding her hand.

Her grip tightened further, "No.. he's out of town...get my mother."

"He's out of town?" Ephraim panicked.

"Mama will know what to do," she winced and squeezed his fingers harder. "Why aren't you going?" she panted.

"My hand needs to go with me," he chuckled lifting her white knuckles to remind her that she had him in a vice grip.

"Oh," she released his hand, "I'm sorry."

He grabbed his hat and headed for the door. Just as he opened it, she cried out in pain and he ran to her.

"Go... no ... don't go. Stay with me," she grabbed his wrist.

"But I don't know what to do. It's not like you're a cow or a mare."

Hannah pointed to Boxer who sat staring at the couple. "Send Boxer for Mama."

"All right," he nodded, "All right." Gently, but firmly he removed Hannah's fingers from his wrist and began his search for a pencil and paper. He jotted the note quickly, placed it in the dog's collar and sent him off to find Anna.

During the next reprieve, Hannah panted, "It's really close. I can feel it."

"What do you mean you can feel it?" Ephraim's eyes filled with worry.

"The baby's there... it's just right there."

"Let's get you into the bedroom before another pain hits," Ephraim lifted Hannah from the couch and carried her into the bedroom. Just as he started a pot of boiling water, Anna burst through the front door with Joshua trailing on her heels.

"Where is she? Where's Hannah?" she exclaimed.

"Back in the bedroom," Ephraim pointed and continued preparing the things they would need for the delivery.

"Oh, I'm so glad you're here," Hannah leaned her head back onto her pillow in relief.

"It's going to be just fine, dear. You'll be holding your baby soon and everything will be all right," Anna assured her daughter with as much calm as she could muster.

Anna was right. Within the hour and after only a few pushes, a beautiful baby girl entered the world. No one could have been prouder than Ephraim. He knelt adoringly next to wife and baby, counting fingers and toes and marveling at how much their little one looked like her mother.

"It's too early to tell who she looks like, honey," Hannah smiled at her husband as he carefully held the baby in his arms and carried her around the room with a slight bounce to his step.

"I tell you she has your blue eyes," he insisted.

"All babies have blue eyes, Ephraim," Anna gently patted her son-in-law's arm and then sat next to Hannah and congratulated her on a job well done.

"What will you name her?" Anna asked.

Hannah looked to Ephraim who answered for her, "Elizabeth Anna Marston."

"Elizabeth was Ephraim's mother's name, and of course Anna is for you," Hannah explained.

Anna smiled and thanked her daughter.

"I wish Father were here to see her," Hannah leaned her head back on the soft pillow and a tear rolled down her cheek. Hannah felt joy and sadness simultaneously - joy for her new little one and sadness that her father had chosen to harden his heart against them. In the process, he'd shut so much happiness out of his life. Hannah no longer held bitterness in her heart, only sadness for her father's loss. She exhaled deeply and closed her eyes, exhausted.

When they heard a knock at the front door, Ephraim peeked his head out the bedroom and called to Joshua, "Could you please get that, Josh?"

Ephraim carried the baby to the window and then back toward the bedroom door. Just as he turned around, he looked up to see Harold Jamison standing in the doorway. Harold's eyes went to his daughter and then to the baby Ephraim held and then back to his daughter.

"May I come in?" he asked nervously.

"Certainly," Ephraim whispered so that he wouldn't wake Hannah.

Mr. Jamison approached his granddaughter and Ephraim pulled back the blanket so he could have a better view.

"She looks like her Mama," Harold noted.

"That she does," Ephraim smiled and then extended the baby toward Harold. "Would you like to hold her?"

"May I?" he asked timidly.

"Take her," Ephraim handed the baby to Harold as Anna and Joshua watched in wonder from the doorway.

Harold rocked the baby gently in his arms, "She's beautiful."

Hannah's eyes fluttered open. Thinking that her father holding the baby was only a dream, she shut them again. But when the vision didn't return, she opened her eyes and saw her once-stubborn father cuddling his granddaughter, his eyes brimming with tears.

"Father?" she whispered.

Harold moved toward her holding the baby. "I'm sorry, sweetheart. Will you ever forgive me?"

"It's already done," Hannah brushed a tear from her cheek and reached out to squeeze her father's hand. He bent over and kissed Hannah's forehead.

Then curling the baby in the crook of his left arm, Harold extended his right hand to Ephraim, "And you? Can you ever find it in your heart to forgive me for all the horrible things I did to you and Hannah?"

Ephraim took his father-in-law's hand in a firm grasp, "Like Hannah said. You're already forgiven. We're just glad to have you here."

As Harold Jamison sat on the edge of Hannah's bed, holding the baby, all trace of sadness fled and Hannah's heart filled with love and joy knowing that the little miracle she and Ephraim had brought into the world had made her family whole again.

About the Story

Hannah's Heart is based on the true story of my great-grandparents, Thaddeus Springfield and Maude Pearson. Maude's parents didn't think Thaddeus was good enough for their daughter. So Thaddeus paid a preacher $50 to marry them in the middle of the road at midnight. Maude's father, William Pearson, was so infuriated that he wouldn't let her come home or let his wife visit her. Maude and her mother, Mary Elizabeth Pearson, kept in touch through notes they sent back and forth in the collar of a dog. When Thaddeus and Maude had their first child, her father's heart softened and the family reunited.

The incident where Hannah sews her wedding dress from a bed sheet was also inspired by Maude who was quite the inventive seamstress. During the depression she created dresses for her daughters from feed sacks that in those days often had flowered prints. Also Thaddeus was a generous and thoughtful neighbor. Like Ephraim in the story, he helped save the lives of his weakened neighbors when a flu epidemic struck. He made soup and carried it around to each of them and helped to nurse them back to health.

If you've read *The Patriot Wore Petticoats*, you'll remember the Springfield name. Thaddeus Springfield was Dicey and Thomas Springfield's great-grandson.

About the Author

Marnie L. Pehrson was born and raised in the Chattanooga, Tennessee area. An avid enthusiast of family history, Marnie integrates elements of the places, people and events of her Southern family and heritage into her historical fiction romances. Marnie's life is steeped in Southern history from the little town of Daisy that she grew up in, to the 24 acres bordering the famous Chickamauga Battlefield upon which her family resides. The Chickamauga Battlefield inspired her book *Rebecca's Reveries* and e-books, *Back in Emily's Arms* and *In Love We Trust*.

Marnie's background is in inspirational works such as *Lord, Are You Sure?* Her first novel, ***The Patriot Wore Petticoats***, is based on the true story of Marnie's heroic fourth great-great grandmother, Laodicea "Daring Dicey" Langston. It was Dicey's remarkable life story and the encouragement from her friend, Marcia Lynn McClure, that persuaded her to step outside her typical inspirational titles to venture into historical fiction. With Marnie's inspirational writing background, you can always count on a moral to every story.

Marnie and her husband Greg live with their six children in Ringgold, Georgia in a house that Marnie designed. You may read more of her work at www.MarniePehrson.com and www.CleanRomanceClub.com or reach her at marnie@pwgroup.com or 706-866-2295.

Other Books by Marnie Pehrson

The Patriot Wore Petticoats
Historical fiction, 224, pages, ISBN: 0-9729750-4-7
Daring "Dicey" Langston, the bold and reckless rider and expert shot, saves her family and an entire village during the American Revolution. Having faced British soldiers, rushing swollen rivers, the "Bloody Scouts," and the barrel of a loaded pistol, nothing had quite prepared this valiant heroine for the heart-pounding exhilaration she'd find in the arms of one brave Patriot. Based on a true story about the author's fourth great-grandmother. Learn more at www.DiceyLangston.com

Rebecca's Reveries
Historical Fiction, 224 pages, paperback, ISBN: 0-9729750-2-0
Rebecca Marchant had led a sheltered life until she found herself inexplicably drawn to the home of her father's youth. Surrounded by the historical landscape of the Chickamauga Battlefield in Georgia, Rebecca finds herself plagued by haunting dreams and vivid visions of Civil War events. As Rebecca walks a mile in another girl's moccasins through her visions and dreams she learns about compassion, forgiveness, temptation and the power of true love.

Beyond the Waterfall
Historical Fiction, 136 pages, paperback, ISBN: 0-9729750-6-3
Jillian Elliott's feet were precariously planted in two worlds: the Cherokee nation on the brink of extermination, and the world where he belonged. On her first meeting with the charming and handsome merchant, Jesse Whitmore had set her young heart ablaze. Yet, could she trust him? Or was he just like all the other white men she'd encountered? Would he stand beside her while she witnessed her nation ripped apart, or would he join the ranks of the powerful greedy to betray her? Inspired by legends and family history of Cherokee treasure hidden along the winding rapids of Georgia and Tennessee.

Waltzing with the Light
Historical fiction, 268 pages, paperback, 0-9729750-5-5
Nestled within the valley of the Appalachian mountains, Daisy,
Tennessee, seemed like a sleepy little town until depression-era
drifter, Jake Elliot, entered it and knocked on the front door of the
yellow farm house and met Mikalah, the oldest of the Ford
children. Little did he know how his life and his heart would be
affected from that moment forward. Although Daisy seems
peaceful and inviting, for a member of the LDS faith it has its
ruthless characters and dangerous moments which threaten Jake
& Mikalah's plans and their very lives. The misconceptions over
Jake's beliefs test the metal of everyone he encounters, bringing
out the best in the most loveable characters and the worst in those
with more treacherous motives.

Lord, Are You Sure?
Inspirational, 152 pages, ISBN 0-9729750-0-4
A roadmap for understanding how Heavenly Father works in
your life, helping you understand why certain problems keep
repeating themselves, how to break the cycle and unlock the
mystery of why you encounter challenges and roadblocks on
roads you felt inspired to travel.

10 Steps to Fulfilling Your Divine Destiny:
A Christian Woman's Guide to
Learning & Living God's Plan for Her
Inspirational, 124 pages, ISBN 0-9676162-1-2
Have you ever said to yourself, "I'd love to do great things with
my life, but I'm just too busy, too untalented, too ordinary, too
afraid, too anything but extraordinary"? Inside this book you'll
learn how to reach your full God-given potential.

To order call 800-524-2307 or visit
www.MarniePehrson.com